The Heimlich
and other maneuvers

A comic novel by
Haskell Barkin

Nonpareil Press

LOS ANGELES

for
Carol

This story is told, in part, through relevant emails. The first of these was sent one day after a fateful morning encounter between two long-time writing partners, Ezra Popkin and Stanley Blitz. The events of that morning would change the course of both their lives.

Ezra to Stanley: My alleged attempt to murder you
How can you think yesterday's kerfuffle in our office was anything but a tragic misunderstanding? How can you not answer my calls? How can you sit mute inside your house while I hammer my fists on your door?

Stanley, you have been my best friend and the finest writing partner a man could wish for. Then yesterday morning, suddenly and without explanation, you quit (both positions, apparently) and reject further contact. So after we have worked together daily for twenty-three years I am suddenly reduced to using email as my only way to reach out to you.

This is not right.

Think of me as humility personified, a Roman emperor kneeling in the snow drifts outside your Encino home, toes frostbitten, seeking only a kind word.

Stanley to Ezra: You want a word?
Here's a great one: ageism.

Our office stinks of futility. We struggled to stay afloat long after it became obvious that anyone who'd have us in to pitch screenplays was, by definition, even more isolated than we were.

There is a mature response—admit our careers are kaput and move on—and an immature response—yours, aka violence.

Luanne and I spent sleepless nights agonizing over my decision. Even then I delayed telling you, knowing that with your short fuse it would be a terrible scene. (Never expected SO terrible!)

Despite preemptive doses of Zantac and Valium my hand shook as I reached for the doorknob outside our office. I would not let you argue me out of it. No matter what you said I would calmly repeat my decision, stand my ground, the way Luanne and I rehearsed it.

Oh, I was prepared for your usual bullying. Nothing prepared me for a barbaric physical assault.

Do not respond.

Ezra to Stanley: Aha!
So we've established that yesterday morning you were both sleep-deprived and drugged out of your mind. Okay, then maybe I was a bit off my game, too. Now let's thrash this out like the old friends we are. Lunch, tomorrow 12:30, Carney's Hot Dog stand. My dime.

Stanley to Ezra: Busy
A real estate person is appraising my house then. Even in this lousy market we should get enough for a comfortable retreat into our Morro Bay weekend place.

Give it up, Ezra. After your mindless attack I could care less about what you have to say.

Ezra to Stanley: Oh the humanity
"I could care less"??!!! Your ragged mental state is no excuse for sloppy writing.

And I never fucking attacked you! My god, Stanley, you march in like a robot (now it's obvious why), eyes glazed, stuttering as you announce out of nowhere you're quitting the business, end of discussion.

The shock hits me like a sucker-punch to the gut.

After which you, my friend, you leapt on me, YOU committed the actual physical attack. Then had the chutzpah to run away screaming, "Bloody murder!"

Really, doesn't that suggest you weren't quite rational?

Stanley to Ezra: A sad case

My god, you actually believe that shit. For the record, I will hereby prick your delusion. Then, dammit, give up, end your harassment, vanish.

I announce I'm retiring. Still typing you say, "Fine, I'll order the gold watch, now let's get to work." I repeat myself. You stand up and beam a chilling glare at me. Cream cheese oozes out between your knuckles from the crushed morning bagel you just took a bite out of. Your eyes grow impossibly wide. You are not breathing.

I leap behind you and pump the Heimlich. You flail like a wild man. I pump harder like the class taught us, until you suddenly wrench back my little finger so far it snaps, sending me into a paroxysm of pain. You throw me down and sit on me, spouting some wild hitleresque diatribe.

I wriggle free and race to the emergency room, where that finger was broken like they never saw before.

I trust this clarifies the situation for you.

Ezra to Stanley: The Heimlich?!!!!

Now you tell me?

I wasn't choking, I was struggling to respond to the professional murder-suicide you sprang on me, but the words stuck in my glottis, dammed up by outrage, disbelief, panic.

Suddenly you're squeezing me in a grip of steel. I grow dizzy. Black polka dots dance in front of my eyes. You squeeze tighter. Now I really can't breathe. Your cure is causing the disease.

It was either your pinkie or my life. (Okay, I'll reimburse your emergency room co-payment.)

My "hitleresque diatribe" was a desperate attempt to get through to what I believed to be my out-of-control best friend.

Stanley, this is Comedy of Errors meets Rashomon! There was a time we'd laugh ourselves silly and then get a story out of it. Because that's what we are, story tellers. Good times and bad, you're a writer like it or not.

Lunch tomorrow, upgrade to the Golden Imperial, still my treat. Where, I remind you, one of the framed 8x10 glossies on the celebrity photo wall is thee and me. Remember how tickled we were when Leland hung us? Writers? On a celebrity wall?

Can you really give up this life?

P.S. I forgive your hair-trigger use of the Heimlich. Since taking the class you're lousy company in restaurants, forever scanning the room, praying for someone's prime rib to take a wrong turn.

Stanley to Ezra: Nothing left to give up
1. In the past three years we've written eleven and 3/4 screenplays. No one has shown the slightest interest. Nothing. Zero. The silence of the grave.

2. The median age of decision-makers is post-pubescent. Their artistic tastes are pre-pubescent. I can't speak for your pubes, but mine are feeling a bit ragged.

3. At month's end our office of seventeen years will be leveled to make way for a car wash. (You want to keep working? Hang around, they'll be hiring. It's your best shot.)

4. That 8x10 glossy is gone. Even Leland Chang knows who's up and who's down. Our replacement is from a reality show.

So here's what I say. Accept reality.

Ezra to Stanley: Sic transit wonton
This reality you speak of, is that you and Luanne stranded in a musty Morro Bay shack for the rest of your days while tempers grow short and the keen edge of your creativity rusts in the damp?

Sure we're having a rough time. But talent and experience not only endure, they prevail. Whoever thinks otherwise is wrong down to the toes of their cute little jammies.

Come on, Stanley, running away is not like you. And certainly not to a Morro Bay weekend place hours from civilization.

Stanley to Ezra: No choice
It's the only weekend place I have. Kindly leave me to it.

Ezra to Stanley: Explain one thing
If we're such hopeless cases, how come our major agency continues to represent us? Fourteen years and counting.

Do you dare question the judgment of Talent Central?

Stanley to Ezra: You're kidding
We've become charity clients.

They keep handing us off to ever more inept junior agents. And with this latest fumbler, somebody's nephew, we've hit rock bottom.

Ezra to Stanley: Unkind
Young Barry may lack guile, but he believes in us, can't wait to get our current screenplay out there. (Three quarters done, partner, almost ready.)

Stanley to Ezra: Tiny problem
Barry doesn't know where "out there" is.

Ezra to Stanley: Even so
He has enthusiasm. He's ambitious. And the kid calls me all the time. How many other agents did that?

Stanley to Ezra: Just our Barry
But only for advice about problems with his weird girlfriend.

Ezra to Stanley: So?
Poor guy has nobody else to talk to.

Stanley to Ezra: Bingo
We have an agent with nobody to talk to. My god, doesn't that tell you something? Come on, when was the last time anyone sent you a check?

Ezra to Stanley: Who knows?
I'm a writer, not an accountant.

Stanley to Ezra: Our accountant died
And that last check came two years ago. Because some cable company in the jungles of Peru ran a sitcom script of ours nonstop for a week. Now, I admire the Incas as much as the next man. But let's face it, they're extinct.

That's our audience, Ezra. An extinct people.

That check's still pinned to our bulletin board. Cash it, see how many egg rolls Leland Chang will sell you for $1.79.

Fade out. The end. I have made my decision.

Ezra to Stanley: Bullshit
At least be honest here. You don't make decisions. Luanne does.

And because you love her and want her to be happy, you gave in knowing it would make you miserable.

I honor and respect you for that. But let's remember that while your wife is kind, charming and intelligent, she is also afflicted with a bag-lady complex. Through good years and bad, Luanne remains convinced that she is doomed to spend her old age on the streets pushing a shopping cart full of cans, bottles and you.

Discuss our temporary slump with her again, emphasize the long view.

Would it help if I spoke to her?

Stanley to Ezra: You're joking
She hasn't forgiven you for breaking my (still throbbing) finger and the aggression that led up to it. But let me guess how she might respond.

She would say how the hell does Ezra know what's best for us? She would scream our financial situations are not the same, no damn way! We're bleeding money every day, but not him, not with Serena's booming architecture business and her celebrity clients up the wazoo.

Some truth there, Ezra. Your wife is a kind, charming, intelligent person and Luanne's best friend. But she's also in a high tax bracket.

Didn't want to bring that up. But goddamn it.

And while we're speaking of marriage, you might consider what's happening to your own. I'm not the only emotional train wreck from pretending he still has a career. Which fucked-upness maybe we both take out on our nearest and dearest.

Or so I hear.

Ezra to Stanley: Lies
Is that what Serena tells Luanne, that I'm the one screwing things up? Obviously my wife fails to mention how her being a workaholic does a pretty good job of pissing out the home fires.

Sad truth is I have no idea what shape my marriage is in because we're rarely home at the same time.

As for Serena's big bucks, cash vanishes faster than it comes in, thanks to that demonic addiction of hers. (Have you been deaf to my kvetching over the years? Or do you think I drive a seventeen-year-old car because I enjoy seeing my mechanic rub his hands together like Simon Legree?)

Please, dear old friend, don't abandon me with such heart-stopping suddenness. We've had too many good years together. At least stay long enough to finish this screenplay.

For the love of God, Montresor.

That night Ezra has an Ambien-fueled nightmare. He is Adam on the Sistine Chapel ceiling, reaching out for the hand of the other guy up there to hold him aloft. The latter turns out to be Stanley in a cheap beard, who extends not a saving hand but the finger. Ezra drops like a stone, ever faster, until he jerks awake, panting, sweat-soaked sheet coiled around him.

Serena wakes up. "What's wrong?"

"A nightmare. Sorry."

"Find a new writing partner. You'll stop having nightmares."

"He doesn't want to do it, you know."

"Leave him alone. You already broke his finger. What were you thinking?"

"Self preservation. I told you how it happened. Why do you believe Luanne's version?"

"I have a busy day tomorrow, Ezra." She rolls over.

"Morro Bay will destroy Stanley. You're the only one who can make her see what she's doing to him."

She mumbles into the pillow, "Forgot to tell you. I'll be in Aspen for a couple of days. Client's first-week grosses are so good she's thinking third story for the ski lodge."

Ezra barely hears this. He's stumbled across a surefire way to keep Stanley in town long enough to lure him back into the fold.

Stanley cannot retire to his house in Morro Bay if said house no longer exists.

Say, for example, it burns down. To Ezra's unmoored 2AM mind the plan seems reasonable. There are no close neighbors. The place is insured—more likely over-insured, considering Luanne's anal approach to finance.

It's old and all wood up to its leaky original shake roof, which dripped water onto the Popkins' pillow when they joined Stanley and Luanne for one of the foursome's seaside weekends, this one a rainy forty-eight hours of bored (yes) games.

How hard could it be to reduce this tinder box to a mound of embers, mold and Scrabble tiles? Stanley has been itching to upgrade the place anyway, a desire Luanne vetoes, reluctant as ever to spend dollar one without a court order. Torching the shack for him would be pure win-win, even a mitzvah.

In his office next morning the cold light of day does what it usually does. Ezra reluctantly abandons his scheme, especially after an internet search reveals the nasty penalties for arson.

Yet the idea intrigues. He toys with it as a purely creative problem, something in a script. After tinkering with it for an hour he concludes only that the Ezra character should not be the one to light the match. Unwise to be seen returning to L.A. after a day's absence with singed eyebrows.

He mentally flits through plots he's written where an honest citizen has to locate a professional to do his dirty work. Fruitless, until the face of a real person suddenly floats before him: Shlomo, the Israeli contractor Serena uses for her remodeling crimes against their own house.

The dreaded Shlomo, whose crew is on constant alert, ready to leap into action holidays or midnight, whenever Serena is inspired yet again to redo home sweet home.

Didn't she mention he used to belong to the Mossad? Hasn't he himself hinted of a danger-filled past?

A quick visit to Morro Bay some moonless night is the least Shlomo can do for him, considering how over the years the Popkins have kept him in shiny new pickups, sent his kids to private schools and financed myriad weekends in Vegas.

Now he recalls—happily—that Shlomo takes an unhealthy glee in the demolition aspect of his work. Two years before, he sledge-hammered his way into their master-bath shower stall to reveal naked Ezra lathering his hair. Shlomo doubled up with laughter, then summoned his crew to share the fun and photo opportunities. Ezra suspects that was the moment Shlomo stopped taking him seriously. So broaching the subject of arson will have to be handled with some tact. But it is doable. Survivor of a thousand story pitches, Ezra knows how to disarm negativity. (Even without turncoat Stanley.)

But time is of the essence, before a buyer appears for Stanley's Encino house.

"It's the truth?" Shlomo asks when Ezra phones. "You crippled your ex-partner with a Tae Kwon Do move?"

"No! Who said that?"

"Dude, you got hidden depths."

"We have to talk."

"So come home. I'm working here again."

The contractor's words trigger a familiar shudder.

Minutes later Ezra's car skids to a stop before his house on a leafy street in the flats of Sherman Oaks. And what a striking house it is. A potpourri of styles, one corner a tribute to Gehry, all swirling polished metal; another displaying Bauhaus austerity; peeking up from the back a post-modern crenellated turret. His wife's addiction in 3-D.

Ezra can't drive onto his driveway because his driveway is being loaded onto a truck. A tractor-like machine with a giant-toothed shovel at one end and giant-toothed Shlomo at the other digs up big chunks of concrete.

Ezra peers slack-jawed through his windshield as the enormous shovel swivels over his car and descends toward the hood, stopping bare millimeters above the metal (give or take a coat of paint). It plucks off a stray branch.

"Impressive, huh?" Shlomo calls down from the cab. "You're not the only guy with talent. Sometime you should try defusing a bomb."

Ezra charges out of his car (delayed by a sticking door that remains unfixed after his mechanic swore success three times). Ezra shouts up over the machine's noise.

"Stop work! Right now!"

Shlomo seems amused by his naiveté. "She's putting in a circular drive. A Japanese garden in the middle. Maybe you could learn to rake sand. Very relaxing for someone so tense."

"We can't afford this!"

"Maybe not you, but your beautiful talented wife, another story. She's also redoing the front entry. And I may have heard the words 'new master suite upstairs'."

"Shlomo, my life is in turmoil. There can be no master suite, no goddamn Japanese garden!"

"Your car sounds like the trunk has bowling balls rolling around. If you're interested the lease is up on my Porsche. Real clean."

Ezra clambers up into the earth-mover's cab and twists the ignition key. The engine hiccups into silence.

"My wife suffers from erectile dysfunction. Don't be an enabler."

"You do not mess with my equipment," Shlomo says grimly. "Be so good as to exit this cab."

"I'm ordering you to leave my house alone."

"Serena orders different."

"I'll work it out with her."

"Sure. And after that come to the Middle East."

Shlomo reaches to turn the ignition key, but Ezra plucks it out, leaps to the ground, stumbles to his car and drives the key to his office.

He ignores his persistent cell on the way. The answering machine at his office blinks angrily.

"Have you lost it completely?" begins the sizzling message from his wife. "You maim Stanley, now sabotage Shlomo's equipment? Enough is enough, Ezra, give the man back his key!"

Ezra calls her. At the sound of his voice she interrupts with, "Look, I realize you're under great stress at the moment. But your writing situation is solvable. So please stop acting out."

Background sounds of nail guns and saws—she's at the Aspen construction site. Despite his anger Ezra imagines Serena wearing that sexy yellow hardhat. Which some day he will ask her to wear to bed, just the hat. If they ever meet in bed again. If he can summon the courage. There was a time when such playfulness (often quite giddy) was a given between them. When did they lose that? How?

"Ezra? Are you there?"

"I didn't mean to hurt Stanley. It was the fog of war. But that is not the subject, Serena. The subject is your new remodel. Absolutely the wrong time. Not now, not when more than ever I need my home to be a quiet retreat from a world run by wailing toddlers and defeatist adults. I will not survive another remodel. Literally."

A careful user of the English language, Ezra does mean literally. After years of life-threatening allergy and asthma attacks triggered by drywall dust, sawdust, paint fumes, wood sap and chain-smoking craftsmen, he feels he has small hope of surviving a new onslaught. Not with his present emotional baggage.

"Okay, I didn't give you warning. I forgot. I'm sorry. That was a mistake."

"Have you also forgotten your unfinished previous remodel? Our entire living room wall is still a drafty sheet of plastic. You tore the wall down seven months ago, Serena! The gas meter lady always catches me lounging in my shorts. It's like I'm working Amsterdam's red-light district."

Serena giggles. "Those sloppy old boxers of yours? She must be getting an eyeful."

"We are not amused. My life is in deep shit."

"For god's sake, just give Shlomo his key. We'll talk this through calmly when I come back."

And the talk starts calmly enough two days later when she returns on a 6PM flight. Through a dinner of delivered pizza that settles in Ezra's stomach like a stone, through an evening of silences and outbursts, to bed time, when he is evicted from the bedroom.

Some highlights of that evening's conversation, starting over the pizza:

Ezra: You swore on a stack of blueprints our house would become a no-architecture zone.

Serena: Promises made under duress don't count. Another slice?

Ezra: Thanks. I forget, was it an Uzi or a pistol I held to your head?

Serena: Worse. It was your month-long sulk after I demo'd the living room wall.

Ezra: So I'm the irrational one? This from someone whose itch to remodel is more urgent than the sex drive?

Serena: Beg your pardon?

Ezra: A figure of speech, for god's sake. Hyperbole.

Serena: I don't think it was.

Ezra: I'm a writer. That's how I express myself. Don't change the subject.

Serena: I hear you shifting blame for our bedroom problems totally onto me.

Ezra: No, no, no, Dr. Fingerman was right, it's mutual. My moody anger plus your vertical-blind ambition.

Serena: Except you never believed that.

Ezra: I believe that going to Fingerman was a waste of time. The man is a total incompetent.

Serena: I remember evenings we came home from therapy and had great sex.

Ezra: Because we laughed ourselves into it by repeating his inane comments. The secret of Dr. Fingerman's success was his deep lack of insight.

Later, brushing teeth, getting ready for bed:

Ezra: Why do you keep torturing our house like this? I want to understand. I really do.

Serena: You write spec scripts? This is my spec script, how I show the world what I can do.

Ezra: Except my scripts don't have someone crouched inside, waiting terrified for the next revision.

Serena: Stop dramatizing.

Ezra: I'm goddamn serious. All I ask for is a dependable quiet place—

Serena: Okay, bottom line. I am not the source of your misery.

Ezra: Our living room wall did not morph into saran wrap all by itself.

Serena: Listen to me, Ezra. You will find a new partner.

Ezra: I don't want a new partner, I just got Stanley broken in.

Serena: You don't have any choice.

Ezra: You think it's easy, like replacing a second story or something?

Serena: For god's sake, there are ten thousand writers in this town, maybe even on this block.

Ezra: Great writing partnerships are made in heaven, like great marriages—though, come to think of it, they're actually made in pre-nups.

Serena: Ezra, denial isn't working. Anger isn't working. Go for acceptance.

Ezra: You know what? You're right.

Serena: Good.

Ezra: I'll work alone.

Serena: Oh, no, no way, you will not!

Ezra: Yes. Henceforth I write solo. The way god intended writers to write.

Serena: Do you understand the chill that sends through me?

Ezra: Not exactly. On a scale of one to ten, ten being the cold reappraisals you give our house—

Serena: Don't be clever now, mister. Not after what you dared to propose.

Ezra: I grant you, once upon a time—

Serena: No. Full stop. Do not imagine for one second you've overcome that old trauma. Not if you care for your sanity and our marriage.

Ezra: Got it. I'm not allowed to veto your career moves even if they turn my home life into chaos. But when the shoe's on the other foot—

Serena: Remember that head-shaped depression in your office plaster? That was when you tried to finish a script alone while Stanley and Luanne toured Europe. And the window you punched out during Stanley's bypass? So much blood—you boasted your stitches out-numbered his. To say nothing about our own arguments, where spilled blood was only seconds away.

Ezra: I never hit you.

Serena: I meant me. Ezra, you're a good writer. But you do not play well without others.

Ezra: Perhaps in the past. I've matured.

Serena: Shlomo and Stanley might disagree.

Ezra: Shlomo scared me shitless with his damned machine! And Stanley attacked me first! Why is my version always irrelevant?

Serena: Look, Stanley has been a safe harbor. You didn't have to deal with that psychic wound of yours. Now, between losing him and a career slowdown, I don't blame you for being scared. But that's no reason to go off the deep end.

Ezra: What've I got to lose?

Serena: Your sanity? Me?

Ezra: A risk we'll both have to take.

Serena: No. I cannot stomach another round of you trying to write by yourself.

Ezra: So this is why I put you through architecture school. To become successful enough to give me ultimatums.

Serena: You'd get that ultimatum if we were living in a mud hut.

Ezra: Wouldn't be a hut long, with that new wing of imported sludge and its thatch-roofed media center.

Serena: Don't do this thing, Ezra. Writing solo turns you into a raging monster who will devour our marriage.

Ezra: (baring teeth) Grrrr!

Serena: You notice I'm not laughing.

Ezra: You notice I'm not joking.

The next morning Ezra plants himself at his computer deter-mined to prove Serena wrong. He opens the screenplay he and Stanley were working on and deletes his ex-partner's name from the title page. Stanley wants out? Out he goes, gone as if he never existed.

He ever comes to his senses, I'll reconsider. I am not a vindictive person.

Ezra jumps to the last page they'd written in their final session before T (for Treachery) Day. Page 78, a substantial two-thirds of a script. All he has to do is toss off the final thirty or so pages. Even at a slothful one page a day he can hand the screenplay to eager Barry in a month.

They were wrestling with how their bad guy might murder the safety inspector of a nuclear energy plant without arousing suspicion. The problem was that any unusual event in that setting would be suspect.

Ezra mounts his stationary bicycle and pedals to stimulate blood flow to his brain. How about we see the inspector walking the catwalk above the reactor. He leans against the railing to look down. It gives way and he lands impaled on a spare fuel rod.

You're kidding, right?, says Ezra Number Two. A fuel rod? Are they even pointy? Or vertical?

Okay, so he just falls three stories onto radioactive concrete.

And the railing gave way because? A bolt pulled loose from the floor? Rust? Come on. Talk about suspicious.

You come up with a better idea.

How's this, the inspector's at home in his kitchen, on a step-stool reaching up to change a bulb. He slips on spilled salad dressing and on the way down his skull slams against the granite counter edge. Or so the police would believe.

Ezra visualizes the man lying there in a spreading pool of blood. Staring up with eyes wide the safety inspector gasps his final words, "You'll never finish it!" The voice is Stanley's.

Ezra now recalls he and Stanley already considered and rejected this way of doing in the inspector. He returns to the computer and stares at page 78 for a long time. Then he googles his name to remind himself that he is an experienced writer. Instead discovers that much of his early career has vanished, though the two other Ezra Popkins are going strong and one Ezekiel Popkin is short-listed for a Mann Booker Prize.

A gob of anger wells up. Why does Stanley let Luanne lead him around by the nose? Screw the son of a bitch, he gets no credit on this screenplay ever, zilch, bupkes.

He looks up "bupkes" to see if it's become standard English yet.

But suppose after the story sells Stanley demands shared credit.

Luanne definitely will push for it. Well, if she wants a fight she'll get it. They won't stand a chance at a Writers Guild arbitration. Ezra will totally eliminate Stanley's contribution to the damned script.

He starts writing the argument he'll submit in arbitration. Too early for specifics, but no harm in having his case ready, with just the right tone of reasonableness and objectivity.

An hour later he has a draft that satisfies him. Now back to the stubbornly un-murdered safety inspector.

Poison? Car accident? Both already considered and dismissed. The son of a bitch will die of old age before Ezra can figure out how to do him in.

Which reminds him that he ought to touch base with his mother in her Boston retirement home. She answers as usual on the tenth ring, with the usual soap opera blasting in the background.

"Hi, mom. It's Ezzie."

"Who?"

Here we go again. "Ezzie. Your son. In Los Angeles?"

No response. He listens to her soap opera for while. Sure enough, they called off the wedding because of that incest thing.

"Mom? You there?"

"Max? Is that you? How are you?"

"I'm not Max, I'm Ezzie."

"Are you sure? You sound like Max."

"Because he's my son. But he never calls you."

"He called me last week from New York."

"That was me. From Los Angeles."

"Did you get the hundred dollars I sent you?"

"Yes. Thank you."

Hold the train. She usually mails him a five-dollar bill "to help with the rent."

"Mom, why did I need a hundred dollars?"

"Oh, Max, you shouldn't be forgetting things at your age. Do crossword puzzles. It really helps you to remember."

"Then remember what the hundred dollars was for."

"T-shirts, I think. Can that be right? They only cost a dollar. That's what I thought you said."

"It's okay, mom. Go back to your TV. Talk to you next week."
He punches in his son's number. Max's latest career move is
hustling bootleg t-shirts at rock concerts. Ezra knows this because
he paid a three-hundred-dollar fine to free the kid from a lockup in
South Carolina, where Max was chased down by the concert pro-
moter himself riding shotgun on a motorcycle.

Did Max learn a lesson from the incident? "He's a billionaire, what's it to him if I sell a few after-market t-shirts?" That
was the lesson.

Ezra prays the phone will not be picked up by one of his son's
interchangeable females.

"Hello, Popkin Criminal Enterprises, Max Popkin speaking."

"You do not go to your grandmother for money."

"Mom was too busy and said you were having a rough time with
Uncle Stanley so I called gramm. I mean, it all comes out of the
same pot, right?"

"That isn't the point. And Stanley has been fired as your uncle."

"Because you broke his nose?"

"Where did you hear that? Your mother? Aunt Luanne?"

"It was on this blog."

"What kind of blog says I broke Stanley's nose?"

"I don't know, like showbiznutcakes.com or something."

"Max, if I hurt Stanley it was in self-defense. Okay? Now, about
your finances. How long do you expect us—"

"Dad, I really don't need The Lecture today."

"Obviously you do."

"No. You'll never have to give me another cent again."

"What's the escape clause?"

"I moved in with this older woman who totally gets me. She's
helping me straighten out my life. Her apartment's at 91st and River-
side, with an incredible view of the George Washington Bridge."

"Older woman? Like how old? Thirty?"

"She turned me on to a career so perfect for me, I mean, it's
crazy to think I never thought of it before."

My son the gigolo? "What might that be?"

"I won't tell you because I don't want to jinx it. But I'm gonna have some awesome news that will make you and mom extremely proud of me."

"Fine, Max. We'll wait for it."

"I do have some leftover T-shirt inventory I owe for. It's only five hundred bucks, but remember you aren't paying my rent anymore."

After promising to transfer the five hundred, soft-touch Ezra locates showbiznutcakes.com, where the only reference to himself is a rumor that he used an earth-mover to wreck buildings in revenge for nude shower photos of himself (see link).

Ten-forty-five. Time for a break. Well, he's earned it, having done some actual writing with his draft of the future arbitration argument. A page is a page.

He drives slowly through his East Hollywood neighborhood to see what new office space might be available. Previous searches with Stanley suggested they had the cheapest square-footage west of the Rockies.

After a while he heads back to the future carwash that is his office, but decides to call it a day instead. He made a start, that's the important thing. Let the inspector's murder marinate overnight and it'll solve itself. Tomorrow he'll write two pages.

Now where to? Going home is the least inviting prospect. (Have sadder words had ever been thought?) He decides to treat himself to an ocean-view lunch and heads west on Pico.

At a stoplight he recognizes the massively bearded leather-clad motorcyclist beside him, an old friend, a producer named Hank Lifshultz.

After a few pleasantries Ezra of course starts to pitch a movie. "We wrote this with you in mind, Hank. Think a polygamist who becomes a cat burglar to get out of the house at night. We call it *Catman Duo.*"

"Tell me more."

But the light changes and Hank zooms off on his Harley.

Half an hour later an excited Ezra is on the phone to Barry, his youthful agent. "So I speed-dialed Hank's cell and raced after him, giving him the pitch over a fast half mile. Son of a bitch fell in love with my idea. Said Stanley and I have the souls of poets. He even came up with an A-list actor he can attach."

"You did all that while he was driving his motorcycle?" says an awed Barry.

"It's a skill. After years of selling my goods to the uninterested, the distracted and the Blackberry obsessed, I am pitch perfect. Hank became so engrossed in my story he drove his bike into the opening door of a parked car some idiot was getting out of."

"Is he all right?"

"A broken arm and lacerations. He told me at the hospital it was worth it, he's fast-tracking our screenplay and expects it to win Lifshultz Productions their next Oscar. As a bonus, Hank promised me two points gross of what he collects from the idiot's insurance for the accident. Barry, I present you with your first big sale."

"Actually, my first sale ever, Ezra."

• • •

Ezra to Stanley: The tide is in
Hank Lifshultz is about to option CATMAN DUO. Details at lunch, you pick the restaurant. Take me for all I'm worth.

Remember, according to the ancient prophets of our people, what keeps this town from imploding into a black hole of bullshit is one honest person. My money's on Hank Lifshultz.

Stanley to Ezra: Nice try
"About to option"? Smoke and mirrors. Get 500k front money, I'll consider.

We had a good run, Ezra, better than most. (Though we did set a record for straight-to-video.) I'd like to think we ended friends. Even if you do tend to break wind under deadline pressure.

Ezra to Stanley: There you go again
I don't break wind, I fart. After twenty-three years, didn't I never teach you how to write direct and simple?

You're okay, too, Stanley, despite your current problem with premature evacuation. The finest, most talented partner a writer could hope for. And the best of friends.

Also you're no fool. Give Lifshultz serious thought.

Stanley to Ezra: I did

Thanks for the kind words. If I ever write a novel you'll be in it, farts and all.

What the hell, you might as well know that when we first met I was so impressed I could hardly stand it. I only had a few *Scooby Doos* under my belt, while you already had a play produced on Broadway. Yet you wanted me to be your writing partner!

I forgive you for using that Broadway credit to pull rank whenever we had creative differences.

Ezra to Stanley: God luv ya

Stanley, I've lied to you for twenty-three years about my New York experience, the shameful truth of which I have until now discussed only with a string of mental hygienists. Sadly, it was far from the shining moment I led you to believe.

Allow me to clear my conscience over lunch. And, okay, I'll even do it at Jerry's Deli, whose pastrami you foolishly find superior to Art's. I'll be waiting for you today at 12:30. And tomorrow. And the day after, aching to spill my guts. (Food quality aside.)

It's one o'clock at Jerry's. For half an hour Ezra has been absently surfing the net on his laptop while fending off an increasingly pushy waitress.

"I'm still expecting a friend," he says as she arrives yet again, pad at the ready.

Suddenly he spots Stanley at the entrance across the room. Yes! He forces himself to concentrate on his computer, where a volcanic eruption is killing beehives somewhere.

A moment later Stanley looms over the table, if someone of his modest height can be said to loom.

"Ezra, this better be good."

"You're the one who likes it here. Up to me, we'd be at Art's."

Stanley sits. "Luanne is pissed because I let you suck me in again. You've really been lying to me for twenty-three years?"

"Every day without fail."

"Okay, tell. What's it about, this shameful revelation of yours?"

"Can we order first before the waitress writes me out of her will? I'm starving. You were a half hour late."

Their pastrami sandwiches arrive with coleslaw, potato salad and baked beans, and the pair dig in.

"Tastier than I expected," Ezra says. "Must be from the north side of the cow."

"Your revelation, please."

"This will be, I warn you, the saddest tale you've ever heard. And you cannot repeat a word to Luanne."

"Don't worry, she's already primed to dismiss it."

"Good. So report it was just what she expected, one of my sleazy tricks."

"Is it?"

"Decide afterwards."

"What is it with you and her? You introduced Luanne to me, you were best man at my wedding, but after all this time I still can't figure out if you even like her."

"What does it take for a guy to confess around here? You want to pass it on to your wife, feel free, let her have a good laugh, but I really don't think it would help matters and I wish you wouldn't."

The waitress tops off their diet Cokes, easy ice, please.

"I started my play in college, where a rough version of it was staged with some success. I moved to New York and kept working on it for a couple of years. The usual starving artist scene, a sixth floor walkup, odd jobs, even hitting up my parents sometimes."

"So Max has a role model."

"You want the story or not?"

"Continue."

"At last I got a production. As I'm feverishly rewriting in the weeks before opening, I have fantasies of fame, of wealth, of entering a new world of sophistication and wit, of all the beautiful women a twenty-four-year-old could handle. But you know what I wanted more than anything?"

"What's left?"

"For *The New Yorker* to mention me in their annual Holiday

Greetings poem. I even imagined what they might write, stuff like, 'To Ezra Popkin, whose dialog pops, a Pulitzer Prize and a toast of schnapps.'"

"Do they still run that holiday poem?"

"Who gives a shit? The point is opening night I was flying high, and the next morning I was suicidal. Every critic in town trashed my play."

"Ezra, I'm sorry. That had to be rough."

"You know me, I pick myself up. Tried to start another play, tinkered with rewrites of the old one. But the spirit was gone. I was desperate for a fresh start in a new place with new people. So I fled to Hollywood on the wings of failure. Met Serena. Met you. The rest you know."

Stanley is perplexed. "That's it?"

"I apologize if my failure isn't up to your standards."

"I'm just saying you were only twenty-four, it was your first time at bat, and you struck out. Painful, obviously, but not a catastrophe. And certainly nothing to be ashamed of."

Ezra produces a brittle, yellowed newspaper clipping.

"I haven't had the courage to look at this review since the morning after my play opened. But last night about 3AM I woke up with a world-class panic attack. The prospect of 'fessing up to you had torn off the scab."

"No scabs, please, I'm eating."

Ezra whispers, "Why the fuck do you think I can't write by myself?"

"You're a sloppy typist who goes postal when you keep making mistakes. Beyond that I have no idea."

"This!" He waves the clipping. "This piece of vindictive shit by the *New York Times'* third-string drama critic. This yellow putrescence which I extracted from the back of my file cabinet last night like an abscessed tooth. Other critics were merely dismissive of my talent. This one hammered it so deep into the ground it hit bedrock." He extends the clipping to Stanley. "I have never shown this to anyone."

"Ezra, the *New York Times* is the Newspaper of Record."

"Read."

Stanley reads the review.

"Oh my god…wow…man, you sure pulled the wool over my eyes. How could I write for so many years with 'an artistically amoral mannerist whose turgid dialog and scant dramatic sense cast over this wasted evening an effluvium of perverted grandiosity'?"

"Are you having fun?"

"I'm sorry but this is so over the top—"

"It's the goddamn *New York Times* with an elite circulation of millions tearing apart a play I poured my life into."

Stanley reads on, fascinated.

"'Among the many overwrought performers, Miss Kelly Greenberg stands out for her total lack of dramatic sensibility. If, as is rumored, the lovely Miss Greenberg is romantically involved with the playwright-director, one can only hope we are merely witnessing his malign influence.' No kidding? I guess being a starving artist wasn't a total loss."

"We shared the floor mattress of my walkup for about a year. Kelly was my best critic as I developed the play, and I coached her acting. We were a great team. But the morning after my play opened she woke up hysterical, after crying half the night, and blamed me for flushing her acting career down the toilet."

"Miss, could we have more pickles here? So? Did she ever make it?"

"Don't you want to wait for your pickles?"

"Our waitress was passing by. I'm listening."

"I encouraged Kelly to keep up with acting classes and auditions. But it was dead between us. I came to L.A. and discovered I could only write with someone else in the room. Far as I know Kelly stayed in New York and vanished into the mists."

"This critic's name, Stefan Jibbet, wasn't the director who won an Oscar last year—"

"Yes, he is that same self-promoting over-praised talent-free knuckle-dragging yahoo."

"Now I get it. And I appreciate your confiding. Even if it did take twenty-three years."

"I'm sorry. It wasn't easy."

"Any chance of reading your play? I can't believe it's so awful."

"I threw all the copies off the Brooklyn Bridge one midnight. Then climbed up on the rail myself."

"You're kidding."

"Of course. I'm here eating inferior pastrami, aren't I? But I came awfully, terribly close." Ezra raises his glass. "So, what the hell, to life, l'chaim, eat up, Stanley there's nothing even this good where you're going."

"I'll come back, we'll fress again every so often."

"Absolutely. Better yet, how about you step up and do a good deed to offset an evil one? Take this final job with Hank to round out my career. It'll be a mitzvah."

"If I did that, Ezra, I swear, I could not go home."

When Ezra returns to his office from the deli a P.S. from Stanley awaits him:

Stanley to Ezra: Truth for truth

I've been hiding something, too, because I didn't want your ridicule.

What I intend to do in Morro Bay is design and build handcrafted furniture to sell at crafts fairs. I sent sketches to a gallery of functional art here in L.A. and they're also interested in showing my stuff when I'm up to speed. So scoff if you like, that's strong validation.

There. Now we're both out of the closet.

Ezra to Stanley: Are you nuts?

Writers who play with sharp tools don't get validated, they only get bloody.

Yes, you have a garage bulging with exotic wood and Teutonic woodworking machinery priced like BMWs, into which you disappear every weekend.

Yes, you bring your latest hand tools to work, exhibiting them to me, the mailman and the pizza guy, as if they were Fabergé eggs. Drill bits made by Rolls Royce ("Ever gets dull, someone personally visits me to replace it."). Chisels hammered by an ancient Japanese who used to forge Samurai swords ("Feel that edge, go on, feel. Oops, sorry, I'll get the Band-Aid.").

But tools and wood are for making things. All you've made is the world's most expensive pile of sawdust. You're no furniture maker, you're a man who loves to collect furniture-making tools.

No, I haven't forgotten the hand-crafted napkin rings you gave us one Christmas. But on this you deep-six a writing career, to schlep around from one county fair to another, existing on corn dogs and deep-fried Snickers bars?

Do not play this cruel trick on yourself.

Come on, before we go our separate ways, let's be two grizzled warriors marching off together for a final adventure!

I'll take Gas-X.

Stanley to Ezra: For the record
Just realized. You always inferred your play was produced on Broadway. According to that review, wasn't it really off-Broadway? Way, way, way off? And two flights down?

Ezra to Stanley: Ouch
Have you no sense of decency, sir, at long last? Must you outrage me with this final affront, failing to distinguish between "infer" and "imply"? I IMPLIED (wrongly, yes) my play was produced on Broadway. But I INFERRED from the reviews that five years of my life had been wasted on a steaming pile of shit. (And reviewed by same.) Okay?

Ah, well, you folks up in Morro Bay must consider such distinctions mere big-city elitism.

Pay attention to important matters, like the precipitous drop in home prices—you can almost hear the little things scream as they plummet. Do you really want to sell now and lose hundreds of thousands? Do you look forward to Luanne complaining forever, "We should have waited"? She will, you know.

There is no response. Ezra commits to an unbroken hour's work on his screenplay, no diversions, no food, no emails, no pee break, all business. To accurately measure this hour he heads for the nearest drugstore, returns with an egg timer and plunks himself down at the computer.

After an agonizing twenty-one minutes he's on the phone with Barry.

"Any word from Hank Lifshultz?"

"Nothing yet. Don't worry, I'm on top of it. Ezra, can you spare a minute? I have a new problem with Bitsy."

Bitsy is the crazy girlfriend. "Actually, I'm in the middle of something, Barry. But what the heck."

"Bitsy wants to make nude pictures of herself as a fund-raiser for an environmental group. I begged her not to, I mean, how will she feel when they show up on YouTube?"

"How?"

"She said that was so typical of me, why I made being twenty-five the new sixty. Ezra, am I really an uptight ivy league drudge?"

"Where'd you go to school?"

"Harvard."

"Could be."

Barry rambles on. Ezra checks his email. Suddenly one message leaps out and starts his heart palpitating.

"Shut up, Barry. I'm forwarding an email to you. Read it!"

Here is the email:

Lifshultz Heating & Air Conditioning to Ezra Popkin: Your marvelous movie

Dear Mr. Popkin,

I have your screenplay, CATMAN DUO sent from Talent Central Artists Management.

My business is Heating & Air Conditioning, so I guess someone made a mistake.

I send this email (it was on your screenplay) because maybe you would appreciate learning of this. Certainly in my business I want to hear when one of my people screws up.

My apologies for keeping your script for a week. But how often does a man like me get to read a movie before it winds up there on the silver screen?

Never, that's how often, which made it a truly moving experience.

However if someone who didn't graduate high school might still make a comment, the scene where your hero and his girlfriend try to resolve their intimate difficulties by dynamiting Mount Rushmore seems unrealistic.

The late Mrs. Lifshultz and I had a similar spat shortly after our marriage sixty-two years ago. We made up in bed with a banana split, but maybe that's why I'm in Heating & Air Conditioning and you're up there telling stars what to say.

Anyway, nothing would give me more pleasure than some day paying eight dollars (senior discount) to see your movie and tell everybody I knew it when.

Sincerely yours, Henry Lifshultz

P.S. Should I return the script to you or your agent? Don't worry about reimbursing the postage, my pleasure. Maybe you'll give me a ticket to the Academy Awards when you win.

"You sent my screenplay to the wrong goddamn Lifshultz," Ezra screams into the phone. "This Lifshultz produces heating and air conditioning. Is there anything about *Catman Duo* that looks like air conditioning to you?"

"I'm so sorry, Ezra. I'll personally deliver a copy right away. It'll be at Lifshultz Productions in half an hour and I'll get a receipt to show you. I swear this will never happen again."

"Okay, Barry, calm down, just do it."

"I don't know what went wrong but I take full responsibility regardless. Or is it irregardless? You once corrected me but I never remember that one. Please don't tell Uncle Brad."

Hardly. This most recent blunder seems only a continuation of the agency's recent indifference to him, bordering on malice. Ezra first noticed it when he learned all his files there had been labeled "deceased" and Brad's apology carried a hint of amusement.

Ezra to Henry Lifshultz, Lifshultz Heating & AC:
Another critic heard from
Thanks for returning my script, after hanging on to it only long enough to read and criticize a story my partner and I rewrote nineteen times.

Maybe some day I can offer advice when a heating job has a problem in the second duct.

Ezra to Henry Lifshultz, Lifshultz Heating & AC: Apologies
Please ignore my inflamed email of thirty seconds ago. I'm going nuts trying to keep my writing partner from jumping ship, and also find a new office.

I'll be happy to pass your firm's name on to my wife. She's an architect with lots of work. Lots and lots and lots.

Henry Lifshultz Productions to Ezra: Huh?
What inflamed email did you send me thirty seconds ago?

As for Stanley wanting to jump ship, I don't blame him. I've had partners who sued me and partners who screwed me, and figured it was the cost of doing business. But water-boarding? (Not that I believe it.) He better forgive you in time for the first rewrite. Must have the golden team, Ezra.

What set you off, anyway? Was he messing with your wife? Were you high on something? (Good stuff? Available?)

Any case, where in hell is screenplay? Already have a VERY BIG actor semi-attached. Or did you give it to somebody else, you sleazy bastard?

Oops, here we go, Clio dropped it on my desk. Ezra, sweetheart, we'll green light this sucker so fast your head will spin. Never again will you have to hustle for your wife.

Ezra to Henry Lifshultz Productions: I am a pacifist
I do not water-board people!

Come on, Hank, you've eaten at my table, attended Max's bar mitzvah. How can you believe these rumors? What's wrong with this town? Must I rent a billboard on the Strip to proclaim my innocence?

Look forward to working with you.

Ezra to Lifshultz Heading & Air Conditioning: Crankiness
Please ignore my ill-tempered email of one hour ago. I'm going nuts trying to find a new office while also struggling to keep my writing partner from jumping ship.

Did you ever have a partner? Did he turn on you?

• • •

Ezra's desperate search for another approach to Stanley (confront Luanne directly?) is interrupted by a curious message from his son:

Max Popkin to Ezra: SOHO's the Food?

Notice the subject, Dad? Happens to be the name of a hot new restaurant, or will be hot once we open. And—ta-da—it's your favorite and only son's new career! Ariadne, my partner, thinks I have the makings of a really great chef.

Our slogan: "International Home Cooking At It's Best."(I know it should be "its" not "it's." But that's how real signs do it.)

Oh, yes. I'm also marrying Ariadne. We tie the knot at Soho's sometime after the hassle of opening settles down. You'll be the first to know the date.

You guys will love her, she totally rocks. Can't wait to book a table for Madame and Monsieur. New restaurant's in this really cool old cast iron building that Mom will go ape over.

Ezra to Max Popkin: Congratulations

Look forward to meeting your Ariadne.

That name reminds me of someone I knew in my NY days. I used to hang out in this Greek diner on Lexington near the 92nd St. Y. There was this gorgeous waitress I lusted after over my moussaka, a dead ringer for an actress a while back named Melina Mercouri . (Netflix her in the classic NEVER ON SUNDAY—they don't make 'em like that anymore.)

Max Popkin to Ezra: Guess what

She's your same Ariadne. Remember you asked me to see if the diner was still there? She inherited the place. Of course from now on all her attention will be on our new restaurant.

Ariadne made me feel like an old friend when I showed up and told her whose son I was. She remembered how you'd sit for hours over a mug of coffee, writing in a notebook (the paper kind—guess you were really poor after all). And how you always "ogled" her when you thought she wasn't looking.

I started in the kitchen doing scut work and some basic cooking and knew in a second this is where I was meant to be. I have a real passion for cooking. Obviously I have a lot to learn and need professional training.

Ariadne's so easy to talk to. Guess she finds me the same. We sit in a booth after closing for hours, telling each other everything.

Hope this makes you and mom as happy as it does me.

Ezra grabs his phone. Max can barely say "hello" before being interrupted.

"Listen to me, Max. If Ariadne returned my ogles she could be your mother today."

"Is this my father the liberal speaking?"

"Hold it—this is a joke, right, the Popkin whimsy gene kicking in?"

"I'm sorry that you find the love of my life amusing."

"Goddammit, Max, what are you thinking? A woman who's my contemporary?"

"Meaning she's as old as you are? In plain English, I mean."

"Don't be snide. Yes. Okay. As old as I am."

"So you're an ageist. Which strikes me as really ironic."

"We're not talking age! It's about differing life experience, perspectives—"

"Something Ariadne and I have already discussed, the whole 'when I'm fifty you'll be 136' crap. We're the best thing that ever happened to each other, so it doesn't make any difference."

"Max, I've been around a bit longer than you and—"

"So has Ariadne, and she's just fine with it."

"I don't question your feelings for her. Nor do I doubt Ariadne's— "

"Nothing I ever do is good enough!" He hangs up.

Nothing good enough? Does Max expect congratulations for his wayward journey since dropping out of college? For holding a dozen jobs (some even legal) in half as many years, ingeniously squeezed in between months of unemployment insurance? For being shocked each month at his roommates' reminder that he's expected yet again to pony up one-quarter of the rent, initiating a jollying email to Dear Old Dad?

And now this farcical move.

Ezra barges past a baker's dozen of hard-working architects into his wife's inner office. Serena looks up from her computer (Ezra thinks he glimpses the Taj Mahal with a post-modern wing) and sighs. He dumps the surreal details of Max's folly onto her. She sighs again.

"Give it time," she says.

"Someone has to go to New York."

"Go."

"Impossible. Hank Lifshultz will commit any second. I have to keep Stanley within striking distance."

"Did you screw her?"

"What? Who?"

"Our son's fiancée. When she was your waitress."

"No. Why?"

"Then we don't have to worry about incest."

"Incest is your major concern? When Max intends to marry someone whose pillow talk will focus on hot flashes?"

"I think it's all very refreshing. Older woman, younger man. I mean, you wouldn't be so upset the other way around, would you? I admire Max for that."

"You're awfully cool about this."

"My actor is suing me for two million dollars because her Aspen house leaks and she doesn't like how it looks anymore. I don't have much worry left over. Leave Max alone. Our son has the attention span of a gnat. Your waitress will be history in a twinkling."

"You already knew."

"He called last week."

"Why didn't you tell me?"

"Because I wanted Max to tell you himself. After all, you were the one who had him check out mementos of your starving artist years."

"Has this become my fault?"

"Hope you didn't tell him to look up that actress you lived with. He may develop a taste for older women."

Ezra stumbles out with the giddy impression that his past is ganging up on him. What mad impulse impelled him to seek Stanley's pity by pulling the scab off that derailed juvenile grab at fame? (And watch those fucking mixed metaphors!)

And now, out of left field, here's mad Max announcing his intent to marry Ariadne of a quarter-century ago.

Who's running this outfit, anyway? I want to talk to a supervisor. The future is terrifying enough, I refuse to put up with the past again.

Back in his office, as Ezra broods over his encroaching past, some welcome come relief pops up among his emails:

Barry, Talent Central, to Ezra: Guidance
You said not to call until I had word about your screenplay. Forgive this email but I am in desperate need of advice.

Remember Bitsy's plan to make nude pictures for an environmental group's fund-raiser? She had me attend the photo shoot to see how trivial nudity was compared to the importance of FETF's mission.

(FETF is Folks for Ethical Treatment of Forests. You might have seen a rogue element on the news because of vandalism, firebombs, etc. They wear ski masks and are pretty paranoid about deforestation. But Bitsy says these people are only a splinter group and FETF must be supported.)

I have to admit that after the first few minutes of photography it really was matter-of-fact. Everyone hanging around the shoot seemed to think so. There was Bitsy naked under the lights, one pose after another, yet they were all busy on their cell phones.

Still I came away feeling more than ever how different we are. She's extremely green, and loves outdoor stuff like mountain climbing and rappelling and cross-country skiing. I'm a committed show business professional and have sinus problems.

But, darn it, I'm totally in love with her! Bitsy's so exhilarating. I don't know what to do. What would you do?

Ezra to Barry, Talent Central: Re Bitsy
Though I know her only by hearsay, Bitsy seems an exceptional young woman with a single-minded commitment to improving the lot of mankind and the Earth upon which it lives.

My advice is to run like hell.

When did you last check in with Hank Lifshultz (the real one)?

"Really, do you have to be such a lying shit?"

This inquiry greets Ezra the next morning as he enters his office. It comes from Stanley's wife. Luanne is at her husband's former desk, emptying its contents variously into a wastebasket and a cardboard carton.

"Disposing of Stanley's remains, I see," Ezra says. "Not man enough to confront me himself?"

"Stanley told me your fairytale version of your New York catastrophe," she says. "What a total, unmitigated fantasy."

"My story, I tell it my way. You want to tell it to him your way, feel free."

Knowing she would not. They were saddled with a secret, a lie, that neither had ever found the right moment to reveal to his or her spouse.

Luanne, of course, was the aspiring actress formerly known as Kelly Greenberg, who shared Ezra's bed in New York. She remained there after he fled, living hand-to-mouth for two more years of rejections by casting directors mitigated by pep talks from her acting coach.

Until the evening she confessed to one of her roommates that if the new guy she was dating that night (advertising, big bucks, says not married but is) took her to a decent restaurant, he could have her for the price of a good meal.

"I'm so tired of going out with actors as poor as I am, who make me spaghetti."

"Our Little Miss Round-heels," the roommate joked.

"Well-fed Miss Round-heels, thank you."

That was when Kelly Greenberg decided New York was over.

The only place she could imagine going was Los Angeles. Raised in a small town in central California, she had always found New York's weather intolerable. Plus L.A. meant movies and television. Not that she would ever wait on tables again or share an apartment with four other hopefuls. But Los Angeles! Life had to be different.

And it's always good to know at least one person in a new place, assuming Ezra was still there.

So Luanne moved into an apartment in a single-story seven-unit stucco building in the Fairfax district with three other girls who were also aspiring. She found work as a coffee shop waitress, where the entire staff knew who was casting what.

She went in search of Ezra. Would he be happy to see her?

Had he made it as a writer? Would he want her back in his life? She found him. He invited her to one of his Sunday lox and bagels brunches at his West Side apartment, where she met Serena, whom he'd married a few months earlier, and a sweetly quiet single guy named Stanley.

Ezra introduced her as someone he had "met once or twice" in New York—there didn't seem much point in revealing an old passion to his new bride. Soon it was too late. Luanne and Stanley hit it off. Ezra and Luanne were stuck with their secret past, which they never mentioned even to each other until now, here in his office.

"The point is, Ezra, I was not the one who became a basket case after those reviews. That person was you."

"Why do women always feel compelled to correct us on minor details, when we're simply massaging the facts to make a better yarn?"

"Because it's a lie?"

"Truth is highly overrated. Great if you're giving directions. But even then who knows what adventures it might lead to?"

"Are you through tap-dancing?"

"Granted, I was in rough shape. Who wouldn't be?"

"You were in worse than 'rough shape.' Suicidal comes to mind. I literally saved your life."

"Literally? Like emergency open-heart surgery? Not that I recall."

"A word to the wise, Ezra: That arrogant tic of yours—correcting other people's use of the language—has not aged well."

"You were certainly grateful back when I helped you sound literate."

"Week after suffocating week you just sat there, curled up like an embryo in that ratty overstuffed chair of yours."

"I was rethinking my future. That chair was where I made decisions." He shook his head in fond memory. "How excited we were to stumble across it on the sidewalk. Schlepped it two blocks and up six flights. I would love to still have that great-armed beast."

"So you could retreat into it bleating, 'I am a black hole of untalented nothingness'? Over and over, driving me crazy. 'Black hole, black hole, baa baa black hole!'"

"An occasional venting does not equal 'over and over'."

"Are you correcting my story on a minor point?"

Ezra snubs her rant to check his computer for emails from Hank or Barry, though he assumes his agent will call the moment good news arrives. Although with Barry you never know, he might just write a letter.

Luanne resumes emptying Stanley's desk.

"Fool that I was, I kept urging you to get back on that horse," she says, "start a new play. Your response? 'I am a black hole of untalented nothingness.' I'd say eat something, a little soup, you have to eat. 'I don't deserve to eat.' I'd wake up frozen in the middle of the night because you'd wrapped yourself in all the blankets. And from the depths of some terrible dream that made your entire body twitch you would groan, 'Nothingness... never...never...never.'"

"Take Stanley's detritus and go away. I have a screenplay to finish."

"When you found you couldn't handle New York one second longer, who got you out of your lease? Me, by telling your landlord a tearful story—reality-based, unfortunately—about how you were on the verge of complete mental collapse."

Luanne turns toward an imaginary landlord. She clasps her hands together and gazes up imploringly.

"Look, Mr. Mancini, look at him sitting there all curled up into himself, he left the gas on yesterday without lighting, almost blew up your building and now he won't even take nourishment. Is this someone you think is going to pay the rent every month?"

Surprising himself, Ezra bursts out with, "Mother of mercy, is this the end of Rico?" The line was a joke between them, his way of suggesting she was overacting.

Luanne stares blankly at him, then laughs with soft appreciation. She is a petite woman with a good figure, especially the upper half, which Ezra still admires when he can get past the tight-ass personality.

If you erase those final weeks, they had a terrific year together in New York.

"I can't figure it out," he says. "You going along with this screwball notion of Stanley's. Making furniture? You will not function well as a pauper."

"We've agreed to give it two years."

"And then?"

She shrugs. "The world's full of possibilities."

"You forgot to add 'la-di-da.'"

"What do you want to hear, that I'm scared shitless?"

"It would be a comfort."

"Okay. I am. And so is he. But this is something he needs to do. So leave him alone, Ezra. Let my Stanley go."

"See you at the county fair, Lu."

"Oh, remember how you encouraged me to sprinkle my conversation with 'fucks' so I'd come across as less pathetically innocent? Well, Ezra, you fuck with Stanley's plans and I'll have your balls for breakfast."

"If memory serves—"

"Go to hell." She hoists the carton and marches out.

Both of them scared shitless? Ezra feels something like joy. He cannot imagine a better state of mind for Luanne & Spouse when Hank's contract requires Stanley's signature.

An email arrives from Ezra's mother at her retirement home in Boston. An event! The first time Mom has ever used the medium.

Ethel Popkin to Ezra Popkin: From your mom
Dear Ezzie,

Minerva, the night receptionist, says all I have to do is type this into her computer and you can read it three seconds later. It's three seconds since I started but I bet you don't have it yet and never will.

Why don't you call me anymore? Why don't you answer my letters?

Your loving mother, Mom

Ezra to Ethel: Congratulations on email
I did get it. See? And now you're getting mine!

I call you every week, but you pick up and then keep watching TV. Most of your letters never reach me, maybe because the letters I do get don't have enough postage. Mom, I have sent you stamps. But try to understand, when the Post Office raises the price of stamps it isn't okay to use up your old ones first.

Better yet, let's email from now on.

Love, Ezzie.

Ethel to Ezra: From your mom
Dear Ezzie,

I don't want you spending what little money you have on stamps, you have to think about how to earn a living now that you're through college. Don't you want to get married and give us grandchildren? Remember, Daddy can always use you in the business. You won't have to work weekends, so you can still write that wonderful play you always talk about.

At least come home from New York sometimes for a visit, we'll send train fare, don't be so proud, you're living six flights up.

Minerva printed on paper the "email" I sent to you and the "email" you sent to me. How come I have both of them? Should I mail one of them to you?

Love, Mom

Ezra to Minerva, Silver Gables: re mom
Thanks for helping my mom with emails.

All the meds she's taking might have side effects that include disorientation. I have tried phoning, emailing and semaphoring her doctor there, but apparently he responds only to Big Pharma and malpractice suits.

Can you tell me what drugs she's on? (The legal stuff, anyway.)

Minerva, Silver Gables to Ezra Popkin: Some people!
Are you asking me to violate your mother's personal space by going through her medicine cabinet, handbag, etc.? Not only is that unethical

and illegal, I consider your request personally insulting. Especially from
a son who never visits.

Let me remind you this is Boston, not Hollywood, where I have a
cousin in the hair styling end of television who says that certain
people are known to pay disadvantaged minorities to run over their
writing partners.

Ezra to Minerva, Silver Gables: Libel
I did not hire people to run over Stanley. I am a good person. I love
my mother. Okay, you have a point, maybe I should visit more often.
Matter of fact I might be dropping in soon, as I may be coming east to
deal with an unwise decision my son has made.

Can you at least assure me that she is functioning reasonably well,
despite minor memory loss and time shifts?

Ezra phones his agent.

"How often have you called Lifshultz today? You have to keep
his feet to the fire."

"I actually went there this morning. Personally."

"Good boy. And—?"

"Mr. Lifshultz took me for a ride on his new motorcycle."

"And—?"

"It has a bigger engine than my car."

"Impressive. And—?"

"Most of it seems used to make noise and vibration."

"The project, Barry. I assume you discussed—?"

"I couldn't catch my breath for the entire length of Mulholland
Drive. Which Mr. Lifshultz unfortunately covered in three minutes
and forty-eight seconds, a personal best even with one arm in a cast.
I'm still shaking."

"And my screenplay, Barry, you did mention it?"

"Of course. Mr. Lifshultz said not to worry, *Catman Duo* is on
track. Plus, the deal now includes a motorcycle at the start of
principal photography, so the two of you can be riding buddies."

"Email that quote to Stanley. But instead of a motorcycle, say
10k worth of woodworking tools. And keep pressing!"

Barry follows up with an email the next afternoon:

Barry, Talent Central, to Ezra:
Re Recent Phone Conversation
I'll do whatever it takes. There's so much to learn around here it's confusing, like my entire four years at Harvard. Everyone says Stanley is entering the Witness Protection Program after you sent him to the emergency room with a broken finger to symbolize what could happen to his leg. Is it true you have contacts in organized crime? Wow! This business is even more amoral than Bitsy says it is.

Uncle Brad says hello, and sends this message:

Word on the street is you assaulted Stanley. Not wise, Ezzie. Showing yourself out of control isn't exactly helpful at this late stage of your career. Bad enough that after the split people will be wondering which one of you was the talent. Incidentally, which one is? Any case, hope you're reunited for Lifshultz because working alone you're a feces-hurling primate. Love.

Ezra to Barry, Talent Central: Only tempted
I DID NOT THREATEN TO BREAK STANLEY'S LEG.

Tell that to your Uncle Brad. And tell him to duck.

Barry, Talent Central, to Ezra: Personal note
Bitsy and I are back together again, but she made me buy a huge number of carbon credits to offset my carbon footprint. I know the Earth is warming up and it's certainly worth a month's pay (theoretical equivalent) to make Bitsy warm up again. But doesn't this seem excessively green to you?

As for Bitsy and I arguing about that nude photo shoot of hers to raise money for FETF, Bitsy kept daring me to make a contribution of my own to the auction. So to keep the peace I let them take some nude shots of me, too. It was terrifically uncomfortable.

Ezra to Barry, Talent Central: Our failing educational system
You write, "as for Bitsy and I." "I?" Me is shocked. Harvard owes you a refund.

Please, please stay on top of CATMAN DUO.

However that matter is soon resolved, if disastrously, by the producer's assistant:

Clio, Lifshultz Productions, to Ezra Popkin: Your screenplay

Hank asked me to thank you for letting us read FATMAN'S DUEL. Unfortunately, it's not the type of property Lifshultz Productions is looking for right now.

A check is in the mail representing your two-point participation in the settlement of Hank's motorcycle accident, which grossed $253,237.17 for pain and suffering in the first week of litigation.

Ezra phones Lifshultz Productions with pounding heart. Hank is unavailable. This is an emergency! Sorry, but I'll see that he gets your message. Where is he? I can't tell you that, Mr. Pritikin. Popkin!! Ezra Popkin!

Ezra phones again later that day and again the next morning. But the slimy son of a bitch continues to avoid him.

Ezra to Hank Lifshultz: Confused

Clio tells me our project is dead. Hard to believe, must be crossed wires somewhere. I have left several messages which obviously never came to your attention.

Anyway, congratulations on getting $253k for your accident. You sent me a check for $19.23. How is that 2% of the gross?

Please get back to me ASAP. Look forward to our being riding buddies.

Hank Lifshultz to Ezra: Sorry for confusion

The $19.23 figure is correct. Your deal was for 2% of the gross, not the gross gross (i.e., after my pain and suffering are relieved, which never comes cheap).

Re your screenplay, what can I say? Actors get attached, they get unattached. A spanking new project comes across my desk, you know me, I have a short attention span.

We'll work together soon, I promise. Maybe not this year, maybe not next year, but we'll always have Paris.

By the way, tell your agent to have a specialist check out his weak bladder. The seat on my new motorcycle was never even out in the rain before.

Ezra is staring bug-eyed at this message when his office door flings open. Stanley stands there with a grimace that rapidly becomes tears. Then he starts sobbing uncontrollably, triggering the same in Ezra.

How could Stanley have learned about Hank's duplicity so fast?

"It's okay, Stanley," Ezra says, patting the shoulder of his sobbing partner. "There will be others."

"Not like Luanne."

"Huh?"

"The worst fight we ever had. Twenty years of marriage, I've never seen her so mad."

"About what?"

"I told her I couldn't abandon you on this final screenplay. You were right. Hank Lifshultz is a straight shooter. Hand-crafted furniture will always be there."

Through a whirlwind of emotions Ezra mumbles, "Absolutely."

"But she'll come around once money changes hands, right?"

"That's our Luanne."

"How soon?"

"Imminent. But you know how negotiations can string out."

"I laid my marriage on the line for you."

"Greater love hath no man. But I worry about Luanne. Go back to Morro Bay and make nice. I'll call the second it happens. Then you can throw bags of gold on the table and leave with love and kisses."

"I can't, I took a stand. Can you put me up tonight? My house here is off limits because they put in rental furniture to help sell it. The agent said our own stuff didn't look like it belonged."

Which is how Stanley winds up sleeping on the office couch (can't have him in the Popkin house, might have to explain to Serena).

The next morning Ezra arrives at his office with coffee, donuts and a list of potential office rentals whose inspection should keep Stanley occupied for days. Meanwhile, Ezra has already phoned Barry.

"It is urgent that you find somebody somewhere to option something of ours for anything. And fast. Stanley's marriage and my scrotum hang in the balance." Silence. "Barry?"

"How do I start?"

"God, you are a slender reed. Okay. Watch the real agents. Rifle through their wastebaskets. Call the people they call. Be a truffle hound, dig, dig, dig, relentless, undistracted. Because you are in a helping profession, entrusted with doing for others what they cannot do for themselves. There is no higher calling."

"Wow. I never looked at it that way."

"Above all, you must reach out to the most connected person you know. Six degrees of separation, shake the hand that shook the hand, follow your access."

"But I don't have any access. Not the least bit. That's why they let me represent you."

"I'm aware of that. But if you'll only stay focused—"

"I'm sorry to be so distracted. But with what Bitsy's been putting me through—"

"Stop. May I speak as a friend?"

"Oh, please."

"I see you lost in the middle of a dark wood, conflicted about which way to go, this path or that one. Night and cold are coming on fast. Big animals out there want to eat you. Yet you refuse to commit to a single path."

"Yes! I feel so inadequate."

"Everybody feels inadequate. Why do you think the world is so fucked up? Barry, I've seen agents come and go—mostly go—but I detect in you a spark of passion that needs only commitment to burst into roaring flame. I believe you have it in you to become one of the greats in the tradition of Swifty, Ari and Lew."

"Me?"

"You. So go forth. Find me an option. And above all remember Stanley must NOT learn that Hank the Shit passed on our project."

"What if he asks me?"

"Lie."

"Lying makes me stutter."

"Sing it to him."

Ezra hangs up with a silent prayer that Barry will, indeed, find his seed of greatness, at least briefly enough to locate one lousy option.

He's tickled by his phrase, "a spark of passion needs only commitment to burst into roaring flame." Somehow familiar. Has he used it before?

Of course! Young Ezra, during his struggle rewriting the final acts of his doomed play, declaimed that creed at a party late one night, to cheers from all and a whopping wet kiss from Kelly, née Luanne.

Now he recalls, with a cringe, that he concluded with the words, "*Ad astra per aspera!* To the stars through assholes!"

God, he hopes Luanne's forgotten all that.

Luanne to Ezra: Bastard
Unbelievable. You sucked in Stanley again. But of course he's only your best friend, so what do you care that you're tearing his marriage apart?

So here's the deal. Send Stanley back to Morro Bay or I will tell both him and Serena all about my misbegotten shack-up with you. In every humiliating—for both you and me—detail.

I'm ready to gamble on the fallout. Are you?

Ezra to Luanne: Bet your ass, Medea
Do your worst. I know Stanley better than you do. He is a forgiving and benign soul.

Except when overwhelmed by your insecurities.

As for Serena, she's known forever about us and has had the good sense to see it for what it was. Namely, less than nothing.

That Serena knows is of course a lie to undermine Luanne's threat, a lie with a bonus. If Luanne even suspects that Serena has known all along about her and Ezra, and said nothing, she has to view every conversation the two women ever had over the years in a new light. Ezra leans back in his chair and savors the thought.

The next morning he arrives at the office with two coffees, his bagel and Stanley's jelly donut. But Stanley is not there. His suitcase is not there. All that is there is an email.

Stanley to Ezra: Fuck you
You filthy lying hypocrite. That you would make a fool of me like this after all these years is beyond contempt.

Correction. Almost beyond.

I have returned to Morro Bay to practice my craft. Never again will I set foot in Los Angeles, that locus of hypocrisy and deception whose prime example is you.

At least Barry has retained some sense of decency.

Do not approach me in any way, electronic or otherwise. I will kill you.

"You have left me without a partner to piss on!" Ezra hisses when Barry answers his phone. "What were you thinking, telling Stanley the truth? Exactly what line of work do you think you're in?"

Barry starts stuttering a semi-hysterical explanation.

"Stop, please," Ezra says, "it's okay, I understand you're not evil, you're just honest. But couldn't you have waited?"

More vocal stumbling on the other end, and then Barry says after a deep breath, "I'm sorry but I have to hang up now." And he does.

Ezra calls back, to be informed that Barry has gone home for the day, if you want to leave a message press the pound your head against the wall.

Ezra is soon contributing to afternoon rush hour traffic, outward bound toward the far, far reaches of the Valley, though both condition and destination are high on his "avoid at all cost" list.

Ezra knows full well that Barry is the weakest link in the chain that holds him above the abyss, and a chill voice whispers that after him there will be no others. Barry has to be apologized to, cajoled, re-inspired and kick-started, with not a moment to waste.

After miles of honking, braking, swearing and being sworn at,

Ezra off-ramps, drives past more auto body shops than there could be cars for, and arrives at a row of older apartment complexes of various designs united only by stucco glitter. A place, he muses, no agent has ever gone before.

The apartment door is opened by a tanned, blonde young woman in full hiking regalia—sturdy boots, multi-pocket shorts and a T-shirt reading "It's Our Planet Too." Her eyes grow wide when Ezra identifies himself and asks for Barry. She throws her arms around him.

"I am so happy to finally meet you!"

Aha. This would be the notorious Bitsy.

"Is Barry around?"

"Irritable bowel syndrome, all that genetically modified food he eats? He'll be out in a minute. Did he tell you how contemptible I once thought you were?"

"Not that I recall."

"Your work reinforces role models that are leading our lemming society over the cliff."

"I try." Taking her in more fully, Ezra appreciates why Barry is so eager to remain with this shapely young woman. He wonders when FETF will be auctioning the nude photos.

"And you were sucking Barry into all that," she goes on. "Oh, how I loathed you."

Barry emerges from the bedroom—more or less, seeming reluctant to share the living room with them. He, too, is a page torn from the REI catalog, in hiking shorts and boots.

"Your backpack is upside down," Bitsy says, rearranging it for him. "We're teaching him to be an outdoorsman.

"I'm sorry I caused so much trouble, Ezra. But I had to tell Stanley the truth. He threatened my life."

"I have trouble imagining 'Stanley' and 'threaten' in the same universe.

"Me, too. Until Tuesday when he came to my office and turned, I don't know, evil."

"Another unlikely adjective."

"He put a polished wooden box on my desk like it was something important, and opened it and took out this dangerous-looking metal weapon thing. He told me, 'The edge on this is un-believably sharp. Things can get pretty bloody if you don't know what you're doing.'"

Bitsy adds, "He bragged it was made by the same French company that used to build the best guillotines. Then he actually forced Barry to run his finger along the edge. It was so sadistic."

"And then he asked me how soon the Lifshultz project would be green-lighted. I didn't dare lie to him. I mean, I'd been managing this lying business pretty well whenever he phoned me. Really proud of that. But now the way he was menacing me I had to tell him the Lifshultz deal was dead, and had been for two weeks."

"Barry said Stanley really went berserk."

Ezra groans. He sinks to the sofa. Reality is slipping away. "It was a goddamn woodworking tool."

Ezra idly assesses the sofa. Arm fabric frayed with a few stains, cushion collapsed. It reminds him of that wonderful overstuffed New York chair. So long ago. When for a moment the world made sense.

"Are you all right?" Bitsy asks.

"Hunky dory, just a little Proustian moment." He says to Barry, "So. We'll talk more tomorrow, right? Regroup, seek out new contacts, keep things moving."

Barry and Bitsy exchange glances.

"What?" Ezra says. "Did our Stanley also perform a black mass? Induct you into the Dark Side?"

"Guess you haven't heard. I left Talent Central."

"No. I can't let you do that."

"I did. The horror is finally over."

"Now that is a rash decision which demands more thought than you've obviously given it. I'm sure your Uncle Brad would be happy—"

"No, Ezra, you were right, I was so in the middle of a dark wood with no clear path in sight. That image of yours forced me to reconsider my entire value system."

Bitsy says, "I could actually sense him growing more enlightened from your selfless guidance."

"I'm no longer driven by blind ambition. Now I truly appreciate how vital FETF's work is to the health of Planet Earth. That's my destiny, the fight Bitsy and I will fight together."

Their deranged bliss signals that further argument will be futile. Ezra flees the apartment before the idiot couple can join hands and burst into a rousing chorus of "This land is my land."

Returning to his office exhausted and aimless, Ezra finds a notice tacked to the door that demolition will start ahead of schedule, at 7AM two days hence.

He rents a pickup truck and Raul, a day laborer standing outside Home Depot, who carries his own large duffle bag full of tools. Desk, chair and file cabinet they schlep into the Popkins' upstairs guest bedroom, the rest into his garage.

Raul's a hard worker and Ezra pays him a bit extra, for which he's immensely grateful. "You think maybe they could use me here?" he asks, referring to the ongoing construction.

"There's the *jefe*. Ask him."

Raul goes to Shlomo, who shrugs an apologetic "no-can-do" and returns to work. A defeated Raul enters the truck to be driven back to Home Depot.

"Not so late," Raul says. "Maybe I'll get another job today. Not everyone has tools."

They drive in silence. After a while Raul removes a chainsaw from his duffel.

"Almost new, real light," he says. "Sell it for a good price."

"Thanks. But I don't need a chainsaw."

"I saw a man carve a telephone pole into a beautiful sculpture with one of these."

"It's for your work."

"Haven't used it for seven months." He shrugs. "I need the rent tomorrow."

"How much?" Ezra says, then adds a ten percent bonus.

Ezra settles into his temporary office in the guest bedroom of his house, a frilly over-decorated room where he collides with one of the twin beds whenever he slides his chair back.

He regrets losing Barry as his agent; he liked the lost kid. Oh, well, Brad will dredge up another damaged soul for him. Except Brad does not respond to his messages. Not the first one, nor the second the next morning. A day later Brad still has not phoned back. Nor the day after that.

"Stop that fucking noise or I'll kill you!" Ezra screams down to one of Shlomo's carpenters who has the temerity to saw a piece of wood. He slams the window shut.

He must endure this room until he locates an affordable office. Preliminary searches suggest he could rent a villa on Capri for the same money locals ask for four walls and a window.

His inbox shows an email from Barry. Come to his senses?

Barry to Ezra: Clarification
I was too embarrassed to tell you the other reason I had to flee Talent Central.

Remember those nude photos Bitsy and I donated to the FETF fundraiser? I finally saw the awful results at the auction. Mine was a life-size print of me lying stretched out, resting on one elbow. I look totally relaxed except for a certain part of me that is horrendously not relaxed. But I swear to you, that part was never originally me.

Trying to calm me down, Bitsy outbid seventeen people for the picture (women and men both!) and burned it. Unfortunately a copy got online, and everyone at Talent Central began looking at me in a different way. Their endless comments and invitations made it urgent that I leave immediately. If that awful photo comes to your attention, please try to understand. It is a photoshop lie.

Bitsy and I have left town on a secret assignment for FETF (Bitsy and me?). Wish I could reveal more.

This communiqué from down the rabbit hole reminds Ezra that he has now been without an agent for three full days, to which he attributes the sudden itchy rash across his shoulders.

He idly types, "If a writer falls in the forest without representation…"

The phone interrupts. Caller ID reveals it's Brad. Ezra's heart leaps.

"Just wanted to let you know how much I appreciate you persuading my favorite nephew to jump ship," Brad says.

"Come on, I busted my ass trying whip the kid into shape."

"Didn't you get the memo, Ezra? Irony is dead. My gratitude is heartfelt. Have to say, I admire your integrity, considering he was your go-to guy here. But perversity's always been your most charming quality."

"I don't get it."

"Remember my witch of a sister, who drinks too much and gets into arguments with my wife? If I didn't hire her baby she threatened to stop visiting our ailing parents and give them my private number. Thanks to you Barry's quit on his own, so I'm off the hook."

"I do what I can."

Brad gives a low chuckle. "If she's still pissed, I'll send her a photo of her kid that'll point up, so to speak, how fast our business corrupts the innocent. You seen that picture? Some fucking genes get all the luck."

"So who do you have for me to work my magic on next?"

"The entire agency. You ever have a project again, we're all here for you."

"I need one specific person, Brad."

"I could assign someone, but they'd never take your calls."

"Why not?"

"Don't make me answer that, we go too far back."

"Picture two men climbing the cooling tower of a nuclear plant, one a terrorist, the other our hero. Way down below the sabotaged cooling pipes threaten to burst, with unthinkable consequences. What could be more timely? *North by Northwest* meets *The China Syndrome*! That's what Stanley and I were working on. Set up a few pitches for me. Somebody will buy this. It's current, a primal fear that the headlines keep stoking. This is good, Brad, you know it is."

"Give me a complete screenplay and we'll talk, which we both know will never happen while you're working alone. So how about

I send you names of some writers looking for partners, okay? Gotta
run now. Wish you all the best, Ezra."

Brad hangs up. Ezra hears a mighty crash under him and the
floor shudders. For a moment he's convinced it's the nervous
breakdown he's been expecting. But he stumbles downstairs to
find the breakfast nook demolished. Workers in the dust remove
broken walls and built-ins.

He hasn't seen Serena for a couple of days. Calls to her cell
have gone to voice mail. Her assistant will reveal only that she is
out of town again.

Ezra to Serena: Emergency
What new hell are you imposing on our house? And where are you?

Serena to Ezra: Sorry
Left you a note on the table in the breakfast nook. Forgot that I told
Shlomo to demo the breakfast nook, which I assume he just did. But
you'll love our new breakfast space. It's a post-modern take on your
favorite architectural landmark, Art's Deli.

I'm up here in Morro Bay, cocooning with Luanne and Stanley.
Absolutely had to give myself some R&R or collapse. Meanwhile can't
help myself, I'm sketching out ways to make this place more or less
livable, maybe even special.

Serena returns after a week but there is little more commu-
nication between them than in her absence. After a few days she's
off on another out-of-towner.

Ezra sits in his guest-bedroom/office with plugs in his ears to mute
the noise of construction and dueling English and Spanish radios.

Now and again he leaves to drive ever-greater distances to
check out office space. He returns home wondering if a two-hour
commute is worth it. Hearing nail guns he wonders if returning
home is worth it.

In the middle of one long, unproductive afternoon at the computer (post nap) a fresh dose of comic relief appears in his in-box:

Barry to Ezra: Hi from up high!
At last I can reveal our plans.

Bitsy and I are occupying a giant redwood tree 100 miles north of San Francisco, to prevent the multi-national logging corporation from chopping down Eric the Red (Bitsy's name for our tree).

They blast military music at us all night long though loudspeakers, but not much reaches up this high. Solar panels recharge our laptop when it's not drizzly and damp, which it is usually.

Our tent takes up most of the space on a wooden platform in the top foliage. It was secretly built by other members of FETF and stocked with enough food and water for months. We climbed up with a rope they left dangling.

It took hours, with only moonlight. Bitsy was incredibly patient, talking me up when I felt I couldn't climb another inch. When I took my first step onto the platform it was like Neil Armstrong must have felt. My arms are still numb but the pain is going away.

The loudspeakers just started blasting tonight's selection, "The Stars and Stripes Forever." Time to put in the earplugs and call it a day. Bitsy says hi.

A few evenings later Ezra awaits delivery of his Chinese dinner, vodka tonic in hand, eyes vaguely on the six-o'clock news. He has forgotten Barry's recent missive until he finds himself looking at a shot of the kid himself side-by-side with one of Bitsy in a debutante's gown. *Shit, they fell out of their damned tree!*

Ezra turns up the sound. No tragedy is being reported, the story is merely about two members of FETF occupying a redwood. The news anchor describes Barry as "one of show biz's major talent agents," and Bitsy as the daughter of P. Bretton Woods, "the Wall Street mover and shaker who invented the hedge fund."

Huh?

Ezra's heart leaps when his feverish internet search reveals that financial innovator P. Bretton Woods is also "a rabid fan of old movies and former owner of a major Hollywood studio." And unbelievably better: "Not merely interested in the financial side of show biz, he is a dreamer who imagines one day 'personally producing, perhaps even directing, a film of my own.'"

Barry has no access to power? Did it never occur to him to glance across the bed at the woman caressing his carbon footprint? And what sort of film is P. Bretton Woods aching to make? Why, here it is, from the mouth of the billionaire himself, "something historical but witty, with a jigger of fantasy."

Thus spake P. Bretton Woods, and therefore is Ezra Popkin reborn twice over, and jubilant.

• • •

Ezra to Barry: Redemption

You wonderful person, you do have access after all, to a modern Howard Hughes no less (though, I assume, without Dragon Lady fingernails). I refer to Bitsy's father.

The man has described exactly the sort of screenplay that would tempt him into production. Luckily, I have such a script squirreled away in my hope chest, FOUR SCORE AND LIFE, a fantasy caper about Lincoln coming back to avenge his assassination. One of Stanley's and my finer efforts.

I want a meeting with P. Bretton Woods. Half an hour, any time, any place. Would you ask Bitsy to do this small favor for me?

I cannot overemphasize the urgency of this.

Barry to Ezra: Mr. Bretton Woods

I'd like to help. But Bitsy's father is one more person I've deeply disappointed.

Once when the three of us were spending a weekend at his country place he took me aside after we watched his all-time favorite movie, BRINGING UP BABY. (He recites the lines with the actors. After one of Cary Grant's speeches he whispered to me, "He did it better last time." He was joking I think.)

Mr. Bretton Woods told me how pleased he was that Bitsy and I were together. She has a lot of Katherine Hepburn in her, he said, and needs someone mundane like me to keep her from going off half-cocked with that environmental crap.

Except here we are living at the top of a giant redwood. Guess who he blames.

Still, I believe I made the right choice. Even if my shoes are moldy.

Ezra to Barry: Weekends at Bretton's?!
Barry, would you mind handing this email to Bitsy? Thanks.

Hi, Bitsy. I appreciate that you have only scorn for what I do. But I did help Barry find his way out of show biz, at great cost to my own career.

However, for better or worse I am still in that business, where the odds are stacked against writers who've been around the block a few times. That, you must agree, is unjust, unfair and pure bias, a clear case of the powerful conspiring to violate the rights of the individual.

I know nothing about redwoods, but I know much about you based on your defense of these helpless giants. You believe deeply in justice for all living things, great and small. I am not great, but I am entitled to earn a small living, am I not?

Tip the scales. Persuade your father to see me. I ask only half an hour of the man's time to pitch my screenplay. Was balancing the scales ever so easy?

Bitsy to Ezra: My Father
You have every right to ask my help, and I'm positive you and daddy would hit it off. He's tremendously fond of creative people.

Unfortunately, it turns out that the multi-national corporation trying to clear-cut Eric the Red and his brethren is controlled by daddy. (Or at least by one of his hedgies.) He refuses to believe it's pure coincidence that FETF has taken a stand in one of his own stands.

I tried to explain that it's not me he's up against, but the earth goddess Gaia. This only made him more furious.

The awful part is he's reached a moment in life when we really ought to get over our differences. Poor daddy's not close to many people, not even my mom or his three other ex-wives. All he has is Magda, his personal attorney-with-benefits, who's a total waste of protoplasm.

Ezra to Bitsy: A helping hand
My son has made a decision that seems as wrong-headed to me as yours does to your father.

Let me speak to him as one disappointed dad to another. My guess is he's eager for a reconciliation, but too proud to make the first move.

I know, totally self-serving. But that needn't stop me from being an honest broker. (Not in your father's league, of course, but with something more valuable at stake than mere dollars.)

Bitsy to Ezra:
You've helped us so much already, I can't ask you to do more.

You only think you need daddy's help. Listen to the deepest part of yourself, Rediscover the wisdom you summoned when you guided Barry out of his morass into enlightenment.

"Fortune cookie advice?" Ezra screams at his computer. "I need life support and she sends me a fucking fortune cookie?"

Ezra types a scathing response delineating Bitsy's mindless preaching, her self-centered take on humanity and her cruel ensnarement of Barry. He deletes it.

Outside all is blissfully quiet: Shlomo & Co. have gone home for the day, doubtless to houses that have never known the scars of saws and hammers. It's now or never, Ezra decides. He will figure out before sundown how his nuclear plant safety inspector dies, or enlist in the nearest monastery.

An hour later he is trying to force-feed his keyboard into the paper shredder. Flying solo, he has as usual flown into a mountain.

Ezra brings up a previously scorned email from Brad's assistant and opens an attachment with a list of writers-without-partners. He phones the first name he recognizes, someone named Peter he's run into at screenings over the years.

Peter seems happy to hear from him. Yes, he, too, is at the moment without a writing partner, sorry about Stanley moving on, and he certainly doesn't believe those awful rumors of violence. Should he?

Ezra starts to consider there might be life after Stanley. Not that anyone could ever be the partner he'd been. The thought inspires him to relate a few Stanley anecdotes. It's only when he chokes up at the climax of one story and there's a dead silence at the other end, that Ezra realizes he's been blabbing on too long.

"So, Peter," Ezra says into the silence, "your ex-partner, what happened there?"

"In a better place."

"Sorry."

"London, precisely. Fred got a play mounted in the West End."

"Good reviews?"

"Raves."

"Wonderful."

"Yeah, pissed me off, too."

"How about we continue this over lunch?"

"I don't think so, Ezra. How you talked about Stanley, that made me realize chemistry is important. I'm going to follow my first impulse, partner up with my son. Youth, that's what the bastards want, right?"

"Oh. Sure. I mean, if your son's a writer—"

"Not really. But the kid's sharp as a tack and has a mouth on him, he'll be great at meetings. And joining the Writers Guild has to be the best bar mitzvah present ever."

A few hours later Ezra calls his wife's cell, which miraculously doesn't send him to voicemail.

"What's wrong?" she says hoarsely.

"I miss you. Where are you?"

"San Francisco. I'm being interviewed for a synagogue addition tomorrow morning and it's 2AM and I need to get back to sleep."

"You have to call off Shlomo. He's closing in on me."

Serena emits a groan that could have reached Los Angeles without cell towers. "Considering what I once had to put up with."

"Beg pardon?"

"Are you really up for this, Ezra? Because I'm groggy and I might say anything."

"That's when you're sexiest. Please."

"Those years you were churning out spec scripts to get a foot in the door? Every day I'd come home from eight hours of minimum wage to a moody, petulant, short-fused writer who just had another script rejected. But did I ever complain?"

"Constantly."

"Then you broke through. Suddenly you and Stanley were hot. I was so thrilled for you, and so damned happy to give up supporting us with that mind-numbing job. What I hadn't counted on was now I wouldn't see you for days at a time. Or when you did come home late and exhausted, you'd be on the phone with Stanley discussing the day's work or tomorrow's meeting. Then you'd take a pill, flop into bed and be snoring in five minutes."

"My recollection is that you had a merry old time running around buying clothes, furniture, jewelry, everything your heart desired."

"My heart desired you, Ezra."

A silence as Ezra tries to catch his breath.

"Sorry," Serena says, "whole truth, I also resented being cut out of the most important part of your life."

"We didn't dare stop working our asses off. It could all vanish.

"How about that. One workaholic to another."

"So you practice architecture as revenge, is that it?"

"You idiot, I'm grateful. You forced me to build a life of my own. I discovered architecture and—wow—it turned out to be something I'm really good at. Now can I go back to sleep? I have a meeting tomorrow with two rabbis and a building committee."

"Sounds like a rock band."

"Thanks. Now I won't be able to keep a straight face. Goodnight."

"Goodnight, Serena."

Next morning Ezra phones another writer from Brad's attachment. However she is no longer desperate to partner, having just sold two screenplays for millions.

"Congratulations," Ezra croaks. "A personal question. Is your age by any chance in the single digits?"

"I don't, like, understand the question."

Ezra spends the next twenty-four hours in a stupor of depression. Even Shlomo's cacophony becomes less of an irritant and more like mood music. He sleeps off and on, has a persistent headache, eats nothing then binges on frosted flakes, graham crackers, hot dogs, whatever the freezer or pantry offer.

During a nap who should appear in an otherwise troubled dream but the good Dr. Fingerman, marriage therapist manqué. He sits at a desk, absorbed in writing something with a quill pen.

"What are you writing," Ezra asks.

"Better the devil you know."

"You're no devil. You're too dull."

The doctor says without looking up, "The moving Fingerman writes and having writ moves on."

Ezra wakes with a start, feeling he has stumbled onto something wonderful. Though he will never again submit himself to sessions with the soporific therapist, he has envisioned an alternate approach wonderfully aligned with his present needs.

And so he phones Dr. Fingerman.

Sorry, the number you have reached is not a working number.

Welcome to the club. But there is an email address.

Ezra to Dr. Sidney Fingerman: Hello again

You may recall patching a rift between me and my wife about six years ago. Your ability to get the job done without prying was impressive.

Life is ganging up on me (career disappearing, partner fleeing, mother failing, wife succeeding). One-on-one confrontations, both professional and personal, have become painful in the extreme. I am loath to walk out the door—any door. Whatever room I happen to be in is where I want to spend the rest of my life.

I pass most of my time (and some wind, according to my ex-partner) busily trying to nap. I wake only to eat, brush my teeth and have a panic attack.

Hope this finds you alive and well. If so, I have an innovative approach to therapy that could benefit both of us.

Dr. Sidney Fingerman to Ezra: Therapy

I do remember counseling you and your talented wife. Please give her my best wishes, if you're still together.

Unfortunately I have moved away from the angst of Los Angeles, to a quiet town where I garden and catch up on a lifetime's list of must-read books.

Attached are the names of Los Angeles area therapists, all experienced and capable.

Ezra to Dr. Sidney Fingerman: Better idea

Don't want capable, want you. Well, you know what I mean, I'm comfortable with you, and comfort has clawed its way up to the top of my Wish List (just above an exploding motorcycle for a certain producer).

Let me propose a method of working together that will barely interfere with your gardening and literary pursuits.

Therapy by email.

What could be less stressful for you than never having to see or hear your patient?

Emailing would imbue our dialog with a greater thoughtfulness—no pressure from the physical presence of the other person in the room, time to compose one's responses more thoughtfully, etc.

You'll make the history books, Dr. Fingerman—your computer will become as iconic as Freud's sofa.

Dr. Sidney Fingerman to Ezra: Alas

Some younger therapist will surely find your proposal irresistible, but fear I'm too old for new tricks. I like my life here in tranquil Morro Bay as it is, without challenge or complication.

Ezra to Dr. Sidney Fingerman: Morro Bay?

You, too? What is that place, the West Coast Branch of the Bermuda Triangle? Beware: If you encounter a man trailing sawdust (and maybe missing a digit or two) he is not the Wizard of Oz Scarecrow. He is a danger to himself and others. Do not turn your back on him.

Please reconsider. I await your response with bated breath. Hurry. I am turning blue.

Dr. Sidney Fingerman to Ezra: Therapy

I attach additional names of local therapists. Urge you obtain help without delay.

The email exchange energizes Ezra. He brings up Brad's attachment with its list of writers seeking partners, and emails or phones everyone on it. A few follow-up lunches result, but produce nothing more than a bloated credit card, a pitch for an annuity that will let him retire in luxury and an invitation to meet someone's widowed mother who is still really hot.

One especially loathsome candidate is an un-bathed, jeans-with-holes, scruffily bearded writer named Zach. What he has going for him is he's in his twenties.

They begin talking projects they're working on, over a vegan lunch. Ezra presents his difficulty murdering the safety inspector.

"Dude, I don't even have to break a sweat for that," Zach says, engendering instant hatred. "Make your guy lactose intolerant and push him into a vat of yogurt. Problem solved."

"We're in a nuclear power plant. Not many vats of yogurt around."

"Does it have to be a nuclear plant? Can't it be a dairy farm?"

"No."

"I don't know, lactose intolerance sets you up for a great love scene with the lady cow wrangler. Like it's late at night, they're on the front porch kissing. She whispers seductively, 'Do you take cream in your coffee? I mean, at breakfast?' and he whispers back, 'Only if you like your men cramped and gassy.' Big laugh, right?"

Arriving home from this wasted encounter, Ezra is buoyed by a new email:

Ralph Bismark, M.D. to Ezra: Partnership
Your email today confuses me. You suggest lunch to investigate forming a partnership. Your accompanying CV consists only of the titles of television shows and films. Am I to understand that you were a consultant on the psychiatric aspects of these works?

I have never considered expanding my practice through a partnership. But if your skill is, indeed, a vital component in the production of films (in this community aren't we all, one way or another!) I would be happy to discuss this matter further. I find no mention of you on any professional roster. What is your training?

Ezra to Ralph Bismark, M.D.: Oops
Sorry, plucked you from the wrong attachment. But I suppose in your line of work you meet people all the time who pluck the wrong attachment.

A big hello from Dr. Fingerman who says please come visit him in Morro Bay. He's so lonely.

* * *

Ezra feels he has regained enough composure to take another crack at the key figure in Operation Rescue Ezra, the lovely Bitsy.

Ezra to Barry: How's it going?

Tell Bitsy I forgive her reluctance to lend a hand in my present crisis. She has already given much in body and spirit to Gaia. If she did that and nothing else it would be enough.

It was selfish of me to ask more of her. Sadly, desperate men do desperate things, and if I'd been able to heal a father-daughter rift along the way, it seemed worth a shot.

I understand how the long view takes over when you're up there high above the frenzied scuttle of life. The greatest good for the greatest number. Perhaps so.

Do you sublet?

Barry to Ezra: Hi

Bitsy's been torturing herself about whether it was right to not help you. Your new email made her cry. If only you were here in person to talk to her, I know you could change her mind.

I'm really lonely. A few FETF climb up once in a while to encourage us and hatch plots but they are not exactly the same as people. A visit from you would do both of us a lot of good. We're starting to get on each other's nerves.

I never climbed a tree before in my life. It really isn't as scary as you think. Come on a Sunday when the forest ranger goons have a day off. A sporting goods store will sell you gloves and climbing spurs for your boots. Shout up and we'll drop the rope.

If I hear the Colonel Bogey March one more time (earplugs are rotting in the damp) I may leap. Not really.

Ezra to Barry: Almost a great idea

But alas, I don't do redwoods. Any idea how long this occupation might last?

Barry to Ezra: Really, really sorry
I never should have suggested you climb our tree. Sometimes I forget
how old you are.

Ezra to Barry: Up yours with spurs
Will ascend on Sunday. Send directions.

By Wednesday Ezra has assembled climbing gear and is raring to
hit the road. With so much time he decides to include a pit stop in
Morro Bay to jolly up Stanley and prime him for the pitch of pitches
that Bitsy is about to initiate.

A soft answer turneth away wrath Ezra instructs himself as he
leaves the freeway at the Morro Bay exit, praying that Stanley's
wrath won't demand more softness than he can muster.

But how can Stanley resist one final chance to be their old
well-oiled team, seasoned pitchers turning on a dime at the least
sign of waning interest, enjoying once again the exhilaration of
snatching victory from the jaws of sharks?

Better yet, how refreshing it will be to perform for P. Bretton
Woods, whose attention deficit, if any, for once can't be blamed on
diaper rash.

He stops in front of a sub-modest house on a small lot four
blocks up from the ocean. With no response to the doorbell, he
removes the key from under its fake rock and enters. Nobody
around. He hears a whine of machinery from the garage.

The garage used to be a dim cobwebby place. Now, standing at
the entrance, he finds it lighted by banks of fluorescents and chock-
full of woodworking equipment.

At the far wall Stanley hunches over a lathe, protected from
sawdust in cap, mask, smock and goggles. Using both hands he
firmly applies a chisel to the edge of a spinning wooden shaft.

Ezra calls from the entrance. "Hi, Gepetto, how's it going?"

Stanley remains absorbed in his labors. Ezra calls out louder.

"Greetings from the locus of corruption!"

Still no response. Spin, spin, scrape, scrape, wood slivers peeling off. Ezra waits for him to take a break. Ten minutes pass. Spin, scrape, spin.

Ezra advances to his work-absorbed ex-partner and gently pulls back one of the headphone hearing protectors.

"I come in peace."

Stanley jerks as if Tasered, jamming his chisel into the spinning wood, which javelins it right back at him. The tool skims a layer of skin from his thumb before shooting across the garage to impale itself in a post on the opposite wall.

Stanley screams, clutches his thumb and turns to discover Ezra standing there with a lame grin.

"Sorry."

Stanley's fixed stare suggests a more conciliatory approach.

"Looks like you could use a band aid. Let me get one."

The far wall holds a white cabinet with a big red cross. Ezra extracts a band aid which he struggles to free from its antiseptic slipcover. The brief red pull-thread breaks off. He tries brute force by gripping one end in his teeth, to no effect except to coat the thing with saliva. He twists it back and forth in growing frustration.

"They call this fucking first aid? A person could bleed to death before you can—" He hears a full-throated roar behind him, the sound hyenas hear when they try to steal a lion's kill, and turns to find Stanley advancing, bloody thumb gripping a six-foot plank. Stanley swings the board wildly at Ezra, missing his head by inches. Ezra runs for his car.

(That particular plank of African bubinga wood will later change the course of both their lives.)

He slams the car door behind him and locks it. Stanley is beating the plank against the car's roof as another car stops at the house and Luanne rushes out.

After a moment's jousting and parrying she's able to lead her husband into the house. With his bloody hand, smock and mask, Stanley reminds Ezra of a deranged tree surgeon.

Luanne emerges a few minutes later and marches to Ezra with fire in her eye.

"As I predicted," Ezra says. "This place has made him crazy."

"Ezra, I have never had reason to ask this. But your relentless pursuit of Stanley begs the question. Have you been gay all along?"

"Is he okay?"

"Why in god's name are you here?"

"I'm headed north to meet my ex-agent and his girlfriend at the top of a giant redwood. Her father happens to be one of America's richest men and he wants to make a movie, and he'll think a certain screenplay your husband and I wrote is the best thing since sliced leveraging. Just wanted to give Stanley a head's up. We may have to move fast."

"Did you say the top of a giant redwood?"

"Is that all you heard?"

"You? How?"

"It's a tree. I climb it."

"*You* climb it?"

"Nobody ever said being a writer was easy."

He drives off. She gazes after him in a new way, anger replaced by a deep sadness.

The last jouncing miles toward Eric the Red take Ezra down an unpaved logging road on which his car rolls and dips like a pirate's galleon in a storm. *More ruts than a Bangkok happy hour,* he thinks, *at least I can find my way back by following that trail of parts dropping off my car.*

Just as Ezra fears some of his own dangling parts may drop off or at least become painfully rearranged, the road ends in a small clearing.

He tugs on his new hiking boots and heads north through the shaded forest floor as instructed. He finds the giant redwoods truly awesome, in the word's original sense (now buried under the crush of teen trivialization).

No question, this is a place worth preserving from the rape of evil clear-cutters. A place so majestic, so transcendent, it might well be able to pull off a showbiz miracle.

Ezra snaps out of his musing to realize he's hiked far enough to work up a sweat, and that one giant redwood looks pretty much like the next. Lost? His GPS seems to agree, as it hunts for a signal, at last finds one and orders him to make his first legal u-turn, then left at the dead stump.

Suddenly there it is in a clearing just off the path, a tree even more grand than its brethren, labeled for easy ID with a yellow tape around its trunk warning POLICE LINE DO NOT CROSS.

The tree is mostly branchless for five or so stories, where the foliage erupts, hiding any view of the squatters above. Ezra phones Barry to announce his arrival, half expecting to be shunted to voicemail. ("I'm not in my tree at the moment, but if you'll…")

Barry answers with overwhelming gratitude. He asks if Ezra enjoyed his trip, isn't the scenery spectacular, did he bring the Oreo cookies? Ezra would be happy to stay there chatting forever, because now that he actually stands before this Costco-sized maypole, the prospect of climbing it strikes him as lunacy.

"Stand back, here comes the rope," Barry says.

A bundle drops from the foliage, unraveling as it tumbles down until the end sways before Ezra like an inverted snake charmer's trick.

No way, Ezra thinks, not a chance. No fucking way in hell.

There comes a time when cosmic seduction overwhelms us. To stand at the edge of the Grand Canyon and imagine the thread of a river below calling us. Afterwards that was the closest Ezra could come to understanding why he changed his mind. Not because above him—frighteningly far above—was the launch pad for his grounded career. Okay, that, too. But, rather, up in the tippy-top of Eric the Red were two people Ezra knew to be totally out of their minds, yet he found himself believing—the magic of the place?— that this stunt of theirs was somehow admirable, even transcendent.

"I'm coming up," he says. "Existentialism lives!"

He dons gloves and spurs, clips on his safety harness, grabs high on the rope (it stretches slightly at his weight) and climbs. Hoist and dig in, dig in and hoist, one step after another, piece of cake.

That is, if a piece of cake would, after several minutes, begin panting like a steam locomotive. Still he climbs, jaw clenched, sweat dripping. After what feels like (though is not) hours his phone rings. He answers, grateful for an excuse to rest and report his progress.

"Hi, Mr. Popkin," he hears, "When was the last time you had your air ducts cleaned out? Dirty ducts can aggravate asthma, nasal irritation—"

Ezra resumes his climb, pushing on despite his machine-gunning heartbeat.

They warned, the people who sold him his gear, never look down, never look up, only straight ahead. But Ezra is bored with the monotony of that view—i.e. bark. He glances up to gauge his progress. How could the treetop still be so far away after all this time and effort?

He risks a quick peek at the ground. His eye is caught by a small black rectangle reflecting the sun. Did he drop his cell phone? Closer inspection reveals that the tiny rectangle is his car. Ezra shudders; he has ascended well above his comfort zone. Shit. One slip and it's all over. Here Lies E. Popkin, A Blot On the Landscape.

He freezes. Can't free his spurs from the bark, can't unclench his hands from the rope, can't move up, can't move down.

And now it starts to rain, a steady drizzle. Of course, he thinks, why not? A soothing sound perhaps under other circumstances but not quite what he wants drowning out his panicky screams for help (soaked cell phone dead to the world).

He listens for a response from his two pals up in their neck of the woods. Nothing comes down except more rain, louder, heavier and, if possible, wetter.

He shivers, soaked to the skin, yearning with heart and soul to be back on the ground.

Though, please, not too fast.

So this is my fate, where it's all been heading, he thinks, to end up as an ornament on a giant Christmas tree. A favorite line of poetry springs to mind: "I'm hysterical. And I'm wet." Never before has he realized how profoundly those words sum up the human condition.

The rope starts to jerk and sway like a live thing trying to shake him loose. Now instead of being unable to free his grip he fights to maintain it against the rope's gyrations.

A voice speaks to Ezra from out of the void. "Who the fuck are you?"

Someone has climbed up below him, a man to judge by the voice. He wears a ski mask.

"Seem to be stuck here," Ezra says.

"I asked a question."

"Name's Ezra Popkin."

"Who's he?"

"Can you help me?"

"You have ID?"

"Not trying to cash a check. Just need help."

"Where are you going?"

"I have a meeting with my agent."

"You don't want to screw with me. Not the position you're in."

"Any chance we hold this conversation on the ground?"

"Know who I am?"

"Little tricky with the ski mask."

"I'll ask you one more time and then you're on your fucking own. Why are you here?"

Ezra helplessly babbles his unabridged autobiography until the stranger shouts "Shut up already!"

Their descent is slow and argumentative due to Ezra's panic. On the ground they are met by two more ski masks who scrutinize his driver's license and question him about the morality of wooden toothpicks.

The interrogation ends at the sound of an approaching vehicle. "Rangers!" cries one of Ezra's new pals. The masked trio scatter, tossing their ski masks.

Soon, as advertised, a pair of men with Smokey-the-bear hats and grim expressions approach him. For a day when nobody was supposed to show up, this is turning out to be a great place to network.

"Thank you," Ezra says. "You have no idea—"

"Sir, do you have identification?" one forest ranger says.

"Look, here's his ski mask," the other says, picking up something.

"Fuckin' FETF bastard," the first one says.

They handcuff Ezra, then radio back and forth a few times to Smoky or someone else, and at last let him go.

• • •

Ezra to Yuri Potemkin, Service manager, Zippo Motors: Screwing

Beware of men with too much time on their hands, Mr. Potemkin. We read everything.

I picked up my car from your shop yesterday, after you repaired steering and suspension damage caused by logging roads.

I notice on your bill for $2372.57 a 5% surcharge "for consumables such as hand cleaner, rags, lubricants, etc." First, let me applaud your restraint in not also charging for toilet paper, the stale donuts in your waiting room and dry cleaning your mechanic's Armani jumpsuit. (Must've brushed against that grease on my steering wheel.)

Some people might consider this 5% mere sleaze, but I know high-concept when I see it. Now I understand where my own career went wrong: My agent negotiated payment for the scripts I wrote, but not the paper they were printed on, ink or carpeting (a consumable: I pace).

Likewise I would expect my dentist to add 5% for that paper bib, mouthwash, cotton wads and drill bits; my doctor 5% for the ice he uses to chill his stethoscope and middle finger.

I am already familiar with yours.

Yuri Potemkin to Ezra: God Bless America

In my former country, the late USSR, 5% for good service would be considered a small peanuts bribe. You should be grateful as I am for living in United States of America where you can take your business elsewhere if displeased.

Would you care to write with me a motion picture of my life? I have adventures that would stand up a hare on back of your neck. We split 50/50.

You do not change your oil often enough.

Ezra to Yuri Potemkin: Thrift, Horatio
You know I cannot take my business elsewhere. The manufacturer has designed my car so the slightest adjustment requires exotic machines that reside only in dealerships.

As for oil changes, why do you assume that if you didn't do it, it never happened? A solipsistic world view, Mr. Potemkin. My oil is drained, environmentally disposed of and refilled every five thousand miles. By me. Personally. Because the name of the game these days is Thrift.

Thanks for offering me 50% of your life but I can barely handle 100% of my own.

Ezra relishes the give and take of their email exchange. If he can write nothing else, this he can do, so at the end of that day blowing his brains out seems slightly less inviting.

With his melancholic yearning and the (metaphorical) pistol waiting in the desk drawer, he imagines himself a character out of Chekhov. To sell the cherry orchard or not, that is the question, and Ezra spends much of the afternoon pondering it.

Then an email arrives, dropping the curtain on Chekhov and opening up a brave new world, with sounding trumpets and a chorus of angels.

• • •

P. Bretton Woods to Ezra: Your Screenplay
Dear Mr. Popkin,

I write at the request of my daughter, who assures me that you are a person of uncommon talent, perception and goodness. While Bitsy tends to go to extremes, I do believe she has inherited my ability to judge character.

She may be mistaken, of course, as I was in believing that her companion in this latest folly would be a positive influence. But I give you the benefit of the doubt; these are dire times and life is nothing if not a gamble. Ultimately, the only truth is ars longa, vita brevis, as I'm sure one in your profession must agree.

In that spirit, would you and your writing partner consider spending an afternoon with me to discuss your screenplay with the delightful name of FOUR SCORE AND LIFE? Bitsy's brief telling of the story has me hooked. Are people still "hooked" in your business?

I'm able to offer an afternoon of undivided attention next Thursday, if you and your partner can fit this into your schedule.

Unfortunately it does require traveling to my country house here in Stockbridge, Massachusetts, which I realize might be a nuisance. Would the use of my personal jet be an inducement?

Sincerely, P. Bretton Woods

Hands trembling, Ezra forwards this email-mirabilis to Brad, stressing that P. Bretton Woods expects the full team, both Ezra and Stanley, and the best person to lure Stanley back is you.

Ezra phones Brad to confirm receipt. To his brain-searing irritation, his words reach only Brad's voicemail. However half an hour later there is a response:

Brad, Talent Central, to Ezra: Nice try
Your P. Bretton Woods letter is brilliant. I'll dine out on it. But don't try more of this shit, it makes you look even more pitiful.

Ezra sends back a steaming email detailing the Barry-Bitsy-Bretton Woods connection, a brief bio of the billionaire and his cinematic dreams and the suggestion that if Brad doesn't persuade Stanley to participate he is the world's most incompetent artist's representative and will be assassinated.

Ezra will also take this to another agency.

Brad phones half an hour later.

"I've looked into it and you have indeed stepped into golden doggy-doo. Matter of fact the timing of this meeting turns out to be luckier than you can imagine."

"How so?"

"Nothing you have to concern yourself with. All you and Stanley have to do is show up and charm the pants off the guy. But remember, P. Bretton Woods is a tad eccentric. Don't let anything he says or does throw you off message."

"And Stanley?"

"Will be there."

Stanley to Ezra: I hate you
Know what you are, Ezra? You're a chutzpa-maniac, a man without a drop of shame in his entire body. Not only do you inveigle Brad to badger me about this latest windmill-tilt of yours, you even suck in Luanne.

I don't need all this psychological warfare. I don't want you in my life anymore. Why can't you leave me alone?

Ezra to Stanley: Because I care
So does this mean you're in?

Stanley to Ezra: Rot in hell
Yes.

On Wednesday at 3AM Ezra, trailed by a sullen Stanley, boards a Gulfstream V at Burbank Airport. Ten minutes later they are airborne, alone in a cabin with dark wood paneling, seats of the softest leather and a fully stocked bar and galley.

"We're in a flying men's club," Ezra observes.

Stanley stares out the window into the dark.

"A cold drink?" No response. "Hey, can you believe this fridge? We could eat for days, never repeat a meal."

Stanley glares at Ezra, then returns to the clouds.

Ezra to Ethel Popkin: Miracles
Dear Mom,

I'm going to western Massachusetts today to meet a producer about a project that will change my life. Tomorrow I'll see you in Boston, then go to New York to see Max.

Stanley and I are flying to our meeting right now, the only passengers on a private jet plane, with a bar and a telephone and a kitchen. How about that? A big electronic map shows what's down below, which is Des Moines, Iowa.

Stanley says hello. A least I think he does. He's been mostly muttering to himself since we left Los Angeles. That will change.

Love, Ezzie

Ethel Popkin to Ezra: From your mom
Dear Ezzie,

How nice to wake up to your message! Can we visit the old neighborhood when you're here? I wonder who's living in our house now. Maybe they'll even let us inside. Wouldn't that be fun?

Everyone is so impressed you're flying in a private jet plane. Minerva told me how many thousands of miles it cost her to upgrade to business class. I can't imagine how many miles you had to use for an airplane all to yourself.

If you call Des Moines from the telephone in the airplane while you're flying over Des Moines, is it still a long distance call?

Love, Mom

Ezra to Ethel Popkin: See you soon
Visiting our old neighborhood isn't a good idea. It may not be safe anymore.

But we'll go anyplace else you want—museums, concerts or maybe just shopping. Start thinking right now about what you want for your birthday, because I'm buying you an early birthday present. Absolutely anything.

And how about this—I'll hire a limousine to drive us everywhere we go. Because that is going to be a day to remember.

Love, Ezzie

Ethel Popkin to Ezra: Worried sick
Why an early birthday present and a limousine? Won't I be around for my real birthday?

What terrible illness do I have you're keeping from me?

Ezra tries to jolly up his dour partner for the entire breadth of the United States, but Stanley remains close-mouthed and distant, nose in a book called *The Woodworker's Guide to Joints*, though Ezra never sees him turn a page.

The plane sets down in western Massachusetts at a country airport surrounded by New England maples. It's just a landing strip, no tower. The pilot explains that the rule for pilots here is simple: "See and be seen, sir."

"Words to live by," Ezra says.

"Call my cell when you're ready for your return flight," the pilot replies from behind mirrored sunglasses.

The writers drive off in the waiting rental car, Stanley at the wheel, Ezra navigating with his phone's GPS. He again reminds his partner that they are certainly receiving star treatment.

"I said I'd do it, and I'm doing it," Stanley replies. "Leave me alone."

After a half-hour's ramble through the Berkshire Hills they arrive at a stone-walled iron-gated enclosure whose brass plaque labels it BRETTON'S WOODS.

Stanley punches in the code their host has entrusted them with. The gate swings open. They drive for a good ten minutes on a gravel road with no structures except giant free-standing abstract sculptures in the middle of meadows.

The house they arrive at is a surprisingly modest New England cottage. Ezra senses something familiar about the place though he can't imagine why.

P. Bretton Woods emerges to greet them. In his early seventies, in tweed jacket and ascot, he seems the epitome of an English country squire.

"Gentlemen, welcome. Thank you for traveling so far to spend time with a lonely old man. I don't usually traffic with writers, but under the circumstances…" He winks.

"Our pleasure, Mr. Woods," says Ezra.

"Please, call me 'P'. Everyone does." P waves them into a rustic living room, where they are soon savoring ice cold beers. This room, too, seems familiar to Ezra, as if he'd been here before. Perhaps a quality imparted by only the most expensive interior decorators?

P breaks the silence. "Bitsy," he muses.

Ezra nods, for want of a better response. P nods back.

"She's something," Ezra finally comes up with.

"Thought she didn't give a damn about me. So involved with her trees. And then her idea that you and I have this meeting—I tell you, it's the sudden small acts of love that truly move the heart. Don't you agree?"

He addresses Stanley, who nods.

"You are so lucky to do what you do," P says. "It must make you very happy."

"By and large," Ezra says. "You know, P, there's something about this room—"

P chuckles. "Familiar, is it?"

"Yes. Why?"

"Cary Grant? Katherine Hepburn?"

The writers are puzzled.

"And a leopard," P adds, eyebrows peaking.

"*Bringing Up Baby!*" Stanley exclaims. He looks around. "This is an exact copy of her aunt's living room in Connecticut!"

"Not a copy, Stanley. The original. At least, the furniture, fireplace, moldings, windows, et cetera. I owned the studio briefly and couldn't resist. Though, I grant you, the house itself is only a copy of the house on the sound stage. The original was rather flimsy for our New England winters. I have it stacked in the garage if you'd care to see it."

"Amazing. I almost expect Cary Grant to walk through that door wearing Hepburn's negligee," Stanley says.

"He did. Well, not in a negligee. Cary spent a weekend here when we were exploring a co-venture. Tried his damnedest to teach me how to cartwheel." He sighs. "I always imagined some day I'd find time to involve myself in the creative side."

"Never too late," notes coy Ezra.

"Bitsy understands my passion. So good of her to make it possible for me to spend this afternoon in the company of professionals like yourselves."

"We are equally delighted to be here," says Ezra.

"Well, then, with bullshit out of the way, shall we plunge into it? How do you gentlemen prefer to work? Characters first? Plot? Do you outline or boldly charge ahead on raw instinct?"

Gesturing with his beer mug, Stanley leans forward in his wingback chair. "Well, P, you might say our approach depends on the specific situation."

To Ezra's great relief, his partner has rejoined the human race.

"It's like shaping a piece of wood," Stanley continues. "You play with it awhile to get the feel of where it wants to go."

"Eclecticism, pragmatism," P says, "exactly how I make decisions. Sign of the true professional. Tell you what. Let's apply the Harvard Business School model to the process."

"Let's," says Ezra. "A bias for action. Focus on the customer—in this case, our protagonist, Mr. Lincoln."

"Works for me," Stanley says. "This is great beer."

"I'll have my brew master send you a case. So. What problems did you encounter with your script? How did you resolve them?"

An insistent knocking cuts short any reply. P excuses himself and opens the front door to reveal a pair of men in white coveralls emblazoned with the name Stockbridge Moving & Transport.

"Ah, me," Bretton sighs. "I wasn't expecting you quite so soon. But please come in. Do what you must."

What they must do (and will for the next two hours) is empty the house of all furniture, appliances, paintings, rugs and even the logs stacked by the fireplace.

"Forgive the intrusion," P says as the movers go about their work. "The Internal Revenue Service will have its pound of flesh."

"Income tax problems?"

"Stanley, you have a gift for understatement. They're auctioning off this entire property. Beware of government employees, gentlemen. They lose all sense of gratitude. I remind those ungrateful weasels exactly who made them wealthy enough to buy their regulatory positions, their seats on the board of governors, their congressional districts. And all they offer is, 'Sorry, P, but in today's political climate,' et cetera." He shakes his head in disgust. "But on to happier matters, this screenplay of ours. What do you call it again?"

"*Four Score and Life*," Ezra says, then warns the mover who has picked up a floor lamp, "Careful with that, it was a favorite of Katherine Hepburn's."

Ezra gives P a conspiratorial wink.

"Who's she?" mutters the mover, "Gavin" according to his

embroidered name.

"You are a poorer man for not knowing," P says, then turns back to his guests. "Yes, the story of Lincoln's revenge on John Wilkes Booth. Strikes me as truly high concept. Isn't that the phrase you people use? High concept?"

P stands to allow the movers to carry out his sofa.

"I know who she is," Gavin says, "I just means, like, you know, who is she?"

"Are you sure this is a good time?" Stanley asks P. "It kind of feels like we're in the way."

"When better?" P says, saving Ezra the trouble of decking Stanley on the spot. "I say we stay with our movie, gentlemen, dedicate ourselves to the work at hand."

P's enthusiasm lights a fire under both writers. Our movie, he said. *Ours.* First person plural possessive, one of those persons being a billionaire. So what if he has tax troubles, these guys always land on their feet.

Stanley and Ezra launch into a pitch as never before.

They are magnificent, even as the house is being stripped bare around them, right down to, as Ezra discovers with chagrin during a bathroom break, the toilet paper. Apparently the *Antiques Roadshow* crowd will value the tp's Cary Grant provenance.

The writers approach the climax of their story. An entranced P looks up from a three-legged stool like an aged kindergartner, until the stool is also carried off and he sits cross-legged on the floor.

Ezra and Stanley hold the stage like seasoned actors. Their voices ring out in a room now emptied down to its wide-plank floor, whose acoustics have improved with each item removed.

They speak alternately, feeding off each other, building to the climax. "Now we're back in the Ford Theatre," Stanley whispers. "Midnight. *Phantom of the Opera* time."

"Silence," whispers Ezra. "Abe emerges from the wings onto the stage. Looks out at the empty house, confused, trying to remember why he's here."

"A growing buzz as people start taking their seats. But—look—it's a twenty-first century audience. Dozens, then hundreds, thousands.

Finally the place is packed. Abe stares out in bewilderment."

"Some scattered clapping at first. But the applause grows until it's like thunder. Whistles pierce the air and a deafening chant of Abe! Abe! Abe!"

"We move in to a tight close-up of his face. Tears run down his cheeks. He understands for the first time that his place in history is secure."

"Abe's face morphs into the granite face of the Lincoln Memorial. Music swells, blasting the triumphant 'Battle Hymn of the Republic'!"

P clambers to his feet, applauding and shouting, "Bravo!" The movers pass through on their final exit, carrying cereal boxes and a light bulbs.

Mover Gavin comments, "Nice concept, guys. Plot-driven but with real characters."

His friend adds, "I see Pacino as Lincoln."

And the movers are out the door, bumping into a pair of federal marshals on their way in.

"Are you P. Bretton Woods?" inquires a marshal.

"I am."

"Under the terms of your surrender agreement—" begins the other.

"I'm ready." P places his hands behind his back to be cuffed. He turns to Ezra and Stanley who watch with mouths agape. "Please, gentlemen, don't rush off on my account. Feel free to make yourselves at home."

"What's going on?" Ezra says in an unnaturally high voice.

"Me, I'm afraid. To a rather pleasant federal facility."

"What for?" says befuddled Stanley.

"Forever," a marshal says. "Your friend screwed the IRS out of about two billion dollars. And counting."

"Do I see tears?" P says to Ezra. "I'm deeply moved. But no need. I look on the days ahead as a time to at last write my memoirs. And thanks to what you've taught me, they'll be brimfull of crackling dialog, conflicted characters and dramatic confrontations."

The marshals lead P to their car. Entering it, he calls back to the distraught pair watching from the house, "May I send you my first draft? Perhaps there's a movie in it."

The car drives off. Stanley begins wailing, "I knew it, I knew it, I knew it!"

"Stop that. You sound like a Jewish Cassandra."

"Shut up," Stanley orders, voice cold as death.

"You think I planned this?"

"Of course not, all you did was follow the advice of a trust-fund baby, the world's worst agent and a Wall Street goniff. What could go wrong?"

"But I was also sucked in—"

"One more word and you're a dead man. No jury will ever convict me."

Stanley sprints to their rental car and speeds off, wheels spitting back gravel. Ezra shouts after him, "Come on, we did this scene already!"

He stands still for a long time, caught like a deer in the tail lights. Then he notices a child's swing, a tire hanging from a tree limb by a rope twisting in the slight end-of-day breeze. The whole setting is so goddamn feel-good American, circa the *Brady Bunch*, that Ezra has to choke back tears.

A seductive thought comes as he struggles for breath. To be swinging from that tree himself, slowly in the cool breeze that has come with the twilight. How lovely that would be, his troubles vanishing like bubbles.

And so he does swing, in the swing, that is. (Yes, that other fatal thought did engage him for a millisecond until he decided he had too much to live for, even if the specifics escaped him at the moment.)

His thoughts range wide as he kicks the dust under the tire.

He could walk into the woods and live off the land.

How easily would that damned house of humiliation burn down? (Should've lit Morro Bay when he had a chance.)

Was this swing also plundered from some movie set? All those trees? The entire fucking ten minutes of driveway?

Darkness settles in. Mosquitoes buzz and bite—another contingent after his blood—and he retreats into the house. He picks up the phone to summon a cab, but the line goes dead in mid-call. He reaches for his cell phone but can't find it, then recalls using it as a GPS in their rental car, where it must still lie as Stanley careers through New England.

The country road that led him here was nothing but miles of woods. To set out on foot at this hour strikes him as an excellent way to never be seen again.

He turns on his laptop for a little light. NO INTERNET CONNECTION it declares. Well, no point trying to call in FEMA.

Bored, but ever the writer, he starts to enter the day's events into his journal until the battery runs out. He fumbles for a wall socket and plugs in the charger, but the electricity is off. Your government thriftily at work.

Bloodies his fist punching the wall.

It looks to be a long night. Especially after he tries to open a window for fresh air and triggers a wailing, whooping, screeching alarm. Terrific, *that* they keep on. Ezra scrambles out before his eardrums are fried and doesn't stop running until the sound is a distant wail that continues for another ten minutes.

He collapses panting to the grass. He doesn't even consider returning to the house. What's the point? He closes his eyes and tries to think happy thoughts.

He's awakened by a man shouting in the distant dark, "Goddammit! The owners are gonna be real pissed at our response time... Because somebody cleaned out the whole fuckin' place... I swear, down to the bare floors, everything except a laptop PC... How the hell do I know, maybe the burglars are Mac people!"

Ezra stumbles through the night toward the voice, reaching P's cottage just as a car with a spinning light on top pulls away. He shouts after it, but the only response is music with a thumping bass as the car vanishes into the darkness.

He curls up shivering in a corner of the porch and quickly falls asleep. In a dream he's floating out to sea on an ice floe and peers back at the receding shore. Nobody is waving goodbye. He wakes to morning light and the sight of a car in the driveway and a plaintive cry from inside the cottage.

"Peeee Baybeee? Peeeee!?"

The cry is Brando shouting for his Stella if Brando were a capon. A woman's voice in pain. Ezra staggers in through the open door to find a bewildered red-haired beauty standing there. She wears a business suit and holds a portfolio.

"P left," Ezra says.

"When?"

"Yesterday. The Feds."

"They weren't supposed to take him until this afternoon."

"Maybe they couldn't wait."

"But I negotiated his surrender for Thursday."

"That was yesterday."

"It was?" She frantically fingers her cell. "Oh shit. Oh fuck. I screwed up again! Fuck, fuck, fuck!"

She runs out. It takes a moment for Ezra's sleepy brain to realize he is about to be abandoned in the woods yet again. He runs after her with a shout that could stop an elephant.

"Hey!!"

Her car is already moving. He runs faster, still calling. She slams on the brakes and he collides with her rear end, pries himself off the trunk lid and stumbles into the passenger seat.

Face scrunched up, she's pounding the steering wheel with her fists. Finally Magda—that's her name—grows tired of abusing the steering wheel. She turns to Ezra as if only now aware of his presence. An unwelcome alien presence.

"Who are you?"

"Me? Only the shmuck your boss flew in to distract him while he was running down the clock."

"P isn't like that!"

"Some of us have a different perspective. Can I hitch a ride?"

"Get out of my car!"

"Okay, maybe I saw him on bad day."

"P is the sweetest, kindest, most thoughtful man ever," she

says, sniffling back tears. "I apologize if you got involved in this. I should have been here on top of things yesterday instead of abandoning him to some…"

"Show biz creep?"

"That isn't what I was going to say."

"I'm numb. Feel free. So. Where are we headed?"

"I have no destination," Magda declares mechanically, as if plagiarized from a GPS. "I have failed in every possible way, as a professional, as his personal attorney, as his lover, as a woman, as a human being."

"I find that hard to believe."

"What the fuck do you know?!" Suddenly Magda lets it all out in one long crying jag, unreeling a series of professional and personal missteps that reach all the way back to teenage embarrassments.

Ezra waits patiently, considering it the price of a ride. But by the time she's sobbed herself out he is rendered less objective than competitive.

"Let me tell you about failure."

He tells her, lubricating his tale with buckets of self-pity. She counters with further examples of her own disastrous life. Then it's his turn again. Back and forth the self-loathing goes, until Magda cries, "Stop, please, no more failure-ping-pong, I can't do this anymore."

They sit staring out in silence past the bird shit on the windshield.

Finally she says, so quietly Ezra can barely hear, "I never really believed P would leave his wife for me. He promised he would, but I didn't believe it."

"Why not?"

"He isn't married. Claimed he was, though. Painted a picture of this world-class bitch who owned everything in her name."

"Cary Grant again."

"Uh huh. What movie was that?"

"You were his personal attorney. How could you not know?"

She starts to cry again, almost inaudibly. He puts his arm around Magda and tries to comfort her. Her tears soak through his shirt.

An extremely erotic sensation, Ezra discovers, but realizing her vulnerability (to say nothing of his own) he stifles the feeling. To his great amazement. There he sits, his real life a continent away, holding lovely Magda, knowing with absolute certainty where they're headed if he allows those tears to have their way with him. Yet he takes the high road.

Granted, he has other motives, like not turning his life into even more shit. His career might resemble Death Valley on a slow day, but at least he has a salvageable marriage and intends to keep it that way.

Magda has driven here from Boston. He asks if he can ride back with her.

"I'm not going back."

"Where are you going?"

"Told you. I don't know."

She agrees to drive him into Stockbridge, informing him en route that ten minutes after passing the bar she realized being a lawyer was a dreadful mistake. That was eight years ago.

In Stockbridge Magda stops in front of the Red Lion Inn. "You should be able to make arrangements here," she says. "Nice meeting you." At which point Ezra has his own epiphany. He does not want to go back to a house in a state of eternal renovation. Doesn't want to sit alone in a guest room/office trying to write without a partner. Doesn't want to wrestle with an industry that scorns him. Does not does not does not.

He suggests they both decompress with an idle day's sight-seeing. Since they're here anyway.

"You mean, like tourists?" she says.

"Exactly. Visit the Norman Rockwell Museum. Check out the shops. Have an ice cream cone. Not think."

"You aren't bummed out by my whining?"

"Gave as good as I got."

Which reminds Ezra of the Seventh Commandment (early draft): Never sleep with a woman whose troubles are worse than your own. *No! Don't go down that road, all you want is to kick back and enjoy innocent pleasures like a normal person!*

"Okay, then," says Magda. "Let's ball."

"What?"

"You're right, let's have a ball!"

That day Magda buys an Aran Isle sweater, a couple of scarves and sheepskin slippers. Ezra cuts a wide swath through a cutlery shop, treating himself to a new pocket knife, corkscrew, stainless steel nose-hair trimmer and the most expensive German tweezers the shop has to offer. This last for Serena, whom her thoughtful husband remembers complaining about her current tweezers. Evening comes and the pair delve further into their life histories over drinks and schnitzel in the cozy cellar pub of the Red Lion Inn. Agree that, by and large, the universe is a rather shabby location.

"I must change my life," Magda says, dipping her spoon into their shared crème brûlée. "Heine."

"Whoona?" is Ezra's two-vodka-tonics answer. Inspiring him to order a self-referential third: "On the rocks with a twist, please."

"Heine. The poet. Or maybe it was Rilke. Said I must change my life."

"How well does he know you?"

"I could practice family law right here in Stockbridge. You know, like that country lawyer Norman Rockwell painted. Help people in ways that count and go to sleep feeling useful."

"I hear he ended up in jail for swindling old ladies out of their life savings."

"Norman Rockwell?"

"The lawyer on the magazine cover."

"I need fresh air."

They emerge into the night. "It's late," she says. "I don't think either one of us should be driving."

"I'll see if they have a couple of rooms," Ezra says. Rooms. Plural. Let the record show.

"Good idea."

But there are no rooms at the Red Lion Inn, something to do with a busload of Austrians. Not likely to find a rooms anywhere, sir, Bavarian invasion.

Magda says, "Anything against sleeping bags? If the sporting goods store is still open, we can buy a couple and sleep in P's house."

Thanks all the same, Ezra thinks, but I'll find a park bench. I'll break a store window and sleep in jail. I'll prop my eyes open with toothpicks.

Says none of the above.

Unfortunately the manager of the sporting goods store has a powerful Yankee work ethic and is thus still open. They buy sleeping bags, a camp lantern and folding toothbrushes and drive back to P's house, most of the time between the lines.

Pitch black inside the house except for their lantern. They climb the stairs.

"Pick your bedroom," Ezra says.

Magda pecks him a kiss. "Your choice."

"I just bought my wife a thirty-two dollar pair of tweezers."

"Plucky."

She kisses him again.

"The finest Solingen steel," he says.

She whispers in his ear, "They know how to make things last. Go on and on."

A man would have to be made of stone to stay on the subject of tweezers, Ezra moans to himself, urgently aware that the description has become all too apropos.

They zip two sleeping bags into one.

He wakes in the morning with elbows, knee-caps and every other protuberance bruised and aching from the night's gymnastics on the wide-plank pine floor. Ezra knows the smart move would be to jump ship, run back to L.A., put this folly behind him. Until his companion opens her eyes and smiles, and he's incapable of making any move at all. Except to jump Magda.

• • •

Ezra to Serena: Greetings from the Berkshires
Doubtless Stanley has told you and Luanne about our misadventure here. I have emailed a slobbering apology to him explaining how I was equally duped though my heart was pure.

I plan to linger here for some desperately needed R&R of my own, the goal being to come to terms with the morass that is my life. Stockbridge has much to offer the frazzled and deflated, besides the internet café where I sit now. Like cheap accommodations—at least if you're squatting in a felon's empty house. No electricity and no furniture, and splitting logs for the fireplace and foraging for nuts and berries at the Price Chopper.

But then again no Shlomo and his wrecking crew. Small price to pay.

It is some consolation that P. Bretton Woods is behind bars. (Must propose an amendment to the Writers Guild contract: Producers who negotiate in bad faith shall do hard time.)

No matter how this turns out, I am trying my damnedest to make things right, though you may at some future point find that hard to believe.

Hope you miss me a little. I shall return. Love.

Did you get the tweezers?

Stanley to Ezra: Pay up
You want to apologize? Send $2229.37 for the last-minute ticket home I had to buy in Boston. When I drove to the landing strip to board our private jet, the pilot told me Los Angeles wasn't on the new owner's flight plan but he'd be happy to give me a lift to Abu Dhabi.

I have taken out a restraining order. Cross the Morro Bay city limits and you'll be arrested.

Ezra to Brad, Talent Central: Manipulative bastard
You unconscionable, sadistic puppet-master, you said my timing was perfect for meeting P. Bretton Woods because you knew!

Were you laughing as you imagined Stanley and me speeding to his country house with visions of Oscars dancing in our heads? Did you giggle at the thought of our pitch playing out to its catastrophic conclusion?

Explain just one thing to me.

WHY THE FUCK DID YOU LET US GO AHEAD WITH THIS?!!!

Brad, Talent Central, to Ezra: Ungrateful child
Try this on for size, Skeezix. How people will talk once the word gets out:

"You know who was meeting with P. Bretton Woods when he did the perp walk? Ezra Popkin."

"Who the hell is that?"

"Popkin the writer, you shmuck!"

"No shit? He operates at that level? Is he available for our project?"

Plus when P. Bretton comes out (and he will) and you are even older and less desirable than you are now, who will he remember as having done him a final act of kindness while he waited for the axe to fall?

But you wouldn't know an act of kindness if it pulled down your pants and made love to you. So let's just call it a day.

Ezra to Dr. Sidney Fingerman: Tap, tap, tap
Hi, doc, it's me down here tossing pebbles at your Windows. I really need that email therapy now. Reconsider. Please.

Attached jottings from my journal detail how I was lured across state lines for immoral purposes.

Plus today my agent emails that I'm suddenly the hottest writer in Hollywood. So of course he's dumping me.

Being agentless at my age (127 in writer years) aborts all endorphins your brain will ever produce. I am the Titanic heading for the Hindenburg—oops—iceberg. (Bear with me; I'm working my way through a case of Bretton Woods Private Label Lager the movers missed.)

This means End of the Line, Dr. Fingerman, a giant gouge in my hull, flames up my gondola.

Meanwhile my wife the second-story lady, like my heartlessly-script-demanding agent, she, too, is suggesting that life without me would not be unbearable.

This from the ingrate I encouraged and suffered with through three years of architecture school, who now despises me because I can no longer hold up my end. How do you hold up an end ripped open by an iceberg?

I love and need this woman, the only person who truly understands me (except for her accusation of self-pity).

Help.

Oh, yes, one more tiny item. I'm sharing my squat and sleeping bag here with a lawyer whose life is also in tatters.

In my business we call that a teaser. Hope you'll sign on for the series. This laptop is my only friend, email therapy my last hope.

Save the endorphins!

Dr. Sidney Fingerman to Ezra: Therapy
The Great Books I planned to read pile up unread. Instead I seek out murder mysteries from the local library or thrift shop, but find myself nodding off after a death or two.

How are Thursdays at three? Email your credit card number and expiration date.

Ezra to Dr. Fingerman: A candle in the darkness
Thursdays at three is fine, as are the other twenty-three hours and six days. My credit card is Amex 0033-4788-9920-0400. My expiration date is any minute now unless we do some heavy lifting fast. Emergency session right now, please, yes?

You know my story up to where Stanley vamoosed from P's house like a cartoon character with steam jetting from his ears. Attached are later pages from my suddenly all-too-lively journal, up to this morning. I love my wife, I do, despite the stress fractures. Magda is just one doozie of a middle-age fling, isn't she? Tell me she is. Please. I'm new at this cheating business.

Ezra to Dr. Fingerman: Hello?
Ten minutes. No response. Answering nature's call? Skipping to the last page of a murder mystery?

Dr. Fingerman to Ezra: Apologies
Must've driven through an underpass during last email. Am now in a supermarket parking lot reading your attachment.

Ezra to Dr. Fingerman: Malpractice
You're negotiating traffic while I zap you my soul? Where is that in the Hypocritical Oaf? Hippocratic Oath. Sorry.

Have I mentioned my son? In his twenties, he plans to marry a woman my age. Should I interfere? He never listens to me anyway and it could make him resent me even more. But I have to try, don't I?

Oh shit. Magda has just strutted in, undressing for me like a stripper. She's fourteen years my junior which, okay, makes me a sexist hypocrite vis-à-vis my son. Least of my worries.

Back to you later. If I'm alive.

Ezra to Dr. Fingerman: Let sleeping bags lie

Thursday at three already. How time flies when you're having Magda. Whose latest "aha!" moment is for us to open our own boutique B&B together. Envisions me as Your Genial Host and breakfast chef, a position for which she refuses to accept that I am laughably ill-suited. She is relentless.

Here's what bothers me. Sometimes I think Why not?

I resist with all my heart and soul, if not my body, but I can't do it alone. Please, Doctor Fingerman, give this hypocritical oaf some ammunition.

It is evening and they lie on the living room floor in their queen-size sleeping bag, enjoying the crackling fire from logs Ezra split and has the blisters to prove it.

Magda is painting her fingernails a phosphorescent red, which, murmurs lust-sated Ezra, remind him of Homer's rosy-fingered dawn. (Then mentally flagellates himself for corruption literary, moral and marital.)

He blows into her ear and whispers urgently, "Opening a B&B tends to be a financial disaster."

"Based on your vast business experience?"

"On the experience of people who fled L.A. for their own B&B dream. Every one came back nasty, brutish and short hundreds of thousands of dollars. It's a faster way to lose money than Las Vegas. Except there you don't have to be charming to strangers as they help you go broke."

"Anecdotal, proves nothing," she says. "I worked up a business plan for an upscale B&B small enough for two people to run with part-time staff. Assuming the right location and enough financing to ride out two years of startup, it'll work. Want to see my spreadsheet?"

"Ready when you are," says Groucho.

"Dammit, Ezra, I hate when people don't take me seriously. P always did. I still have his power-of-attorney to tie up loose ends. And watch it."

"You have his power of attorney?"

"A limited power. Why?"

"Enough to maybe turn on electricity here?"

"Oh. Never thought of that," she says sheepishly. "Fucked up again, huh?"

Next day her limited power of attorney does the trick and they emerge from the third world. Ezra reciprocates by using his power of idiocy (unlimited) to buy a microwave and rent a fridge, which she takes to mean commitment.

That evening over frozen pizza the subject of the B&B comes up again. He reminds her that his marriage is far from over, but she counters with a statistic he let slip while drooling with passion, that he's had more sex in the past week than the previous six months.

She also points out that if he transforms himself into a B&B host he will never again have to set finger to keyboard.

"Why would I want that?"

"Because whenever you talk about writing a big vein starts throbbing in your forehead."

"Part of the job description."

"Stanley's smarter than you are."

"Magda, I cannot invest in your B&B even if I wanted to. I have dwindling assets, a couple of mortgages demanding their monthly vigorish and a contractor my wife has adopted."

"Money is not an issue. P made me rich. He financed my participation in one of his transactions."

"Oh, shit, are they coming after you, too?"

"I got out before he went off the deep end."

"When you say 'rich'—?"

"Tens of millions."

"All quite legal?"

She gazes around the room. "Ezra—the perfect house for our B&B is right here! I know P would love me to be the new owner."

"Know what he'd love even more? Seeing my screenplay produced." At her stony glare Ezra adds, "Not that we couldn't multi-task."

"And I thought the most self-destructive person I knew was me. Oh, let go, baby, let all that go."

God help me, thinks Ezra, the scale is tipping.

In his next private moment he sends Dr. Fingerman an urgent email, updating his emotional state and begging for immediate emergency guidance. It's a long half day before the response comes.

Dr. Fingerman to Ezra: Your McGuffin

Sorry for the delay. I was at my evening class on Cinema at our local college, which I attend to occupy some of my many empty hours here in Morro Bay.

The subject last night was Alfred Hitchcock's "McGuffin," a thing that motivates characters but is intrinsically worthless.

I believe your personal McGuffin is that play you wrote in your twenties. It does appear to drive the plot of your life. Managing a B&B may seem an escape, but Mr. McGuffin will always want a room.

(Your former writing partner lectured a week ago. His subject was "Screenwriting: A False God." He found a number of parallels between writing scripts and the design and construction of furniture, to the detriment of script writing. He seems quite bitter.)

How are house prices in Stockbridge?

Ezra to Dr. Fingerman: All bets off

Magda grew increasingly insistent about the B&B thing. To placate her I enrolled in a local cooking school, majoring in Breakfast, though I am the last person yawning guests want to find in the AM assembling their Eggs Benedict Arnold.

I'm not sure if I was stringing her along or backing into a new life while denying it. Then suddenly events were in the saddle and the decision was out of my hands.

I was doing my homework, boiling eggs by the dozen (soft, hard, medium), when a pickup labeled "Ed's Quality Construction." pulled up outside. Magda eagerly welcomed two men wearing tool belts. One unrolled a set of blueprints on the floor. Another began taking test swings with a sledgehammer at the kitchen wall.

Magda shouted to me over the noise, "Some friends of P's say no need to wait for the auction, the place is mine if I want it. Might as well get started with the remodel!"

I snapped. Your classic Pavlovian response. Irrational, of course. Because why shouldn't Magda rebuild to convert the place into a B&B? I see that now. But at the time I went completely bonkers, said things one should not say to someone with a fragile ego. As did she, who screamed the hell with me, she'd go it alone, didn't need her life screwed up by another self-involved man/boy.

Why do women do this to us? Are they equipped with a set of remodeling genes—we have testicles, they have wrecking balls?

So it's back to L.A., with stops in New York and then Boston, places various relatives require my steadying hand.

Massive adulterous guilt is creeping up on me. Can I face Serena without blurting out, "You know, a funny thing happened after Stanley stranded me in Stockbridge...?"

P.S. Re local real estate, I can put you into the Old Freud Place for a million-five. They say Oedipus slept there. It's a site for sore eyes.

• • •

Ezra to Max Popkin: Big daddy's comin'
Will arrive in NY tomorrow. Where and when can we get together?

Ariadne Koppos to Ezra: After all these years
Have dinner at our apartment tomorrow night, seven o'clock. Max will be our chef. You'll be pleasantly surprised. He's a rare talent.

I know I'm a less pleasant surprise. Can we become reacquainted before you make a judgment?

If you're anything like your son, I was a fool to ignore your love-smitten glances all those years ago (oh, yes, I noticed them), and your attempts to impress me with comments on culture and art that were way over my head.

Max and I are both exhausted from putting together the new restaurant. We leave Monday for three weeks in the Greek Islands, because once we open our doors there won't be any getting away for a long time.

A confession: Remember you once left your notebook behind at the diner? I couldn't resist reading it because you oh-so-casually mentioned you were writing a play that would change the course of American theatre. I couldn't make heads or tails of all that intellectual dialog, but I was impressed.

Did you forget that notebook on purpose? I think you did.

I once read a story with an unforgettable opening line: "After all those years she saw him again." Kind of what I'm feeling.

Ezra to Serena: My dinner with Ariadne

Our son cooked a delicious five-course meal for me. The kid knows what he's doing.

Later when we were all feeling mellow I took him aside and tried to reason with him, adopting my most fatherly manner. He reasoned right back at me with the calm assurance of the true believer. All in all, a warm if unproductive heart-to-heart.

They'll be in Greece for the next three weeks to see her family. Well, nothing like travel to shatter a relationship.

Otherwise plan on gaining not only a daughter-in-law, but two step-grandchildren, a boy and girl. They're precocious little tykes—she's an orthodontist, he runs an art gallery with paintings by the deranged. (A useful contact if I change careers.)

I have the use of the apartment while they're away.

Ezra to Dr. Fingerman: Alone at last

My son Max cooked a delicious five-course meal for me.

Later I took Max aside for a father-son talk about his significantly older other. Leading to a knock-down-drag-out argument in which he accused me of lusting after her myself.

His repugnant charge was, needless to say, right on the money. But only in the way that any man will lust after any attractive woman. Especially one he had a crush on a few decades ago, now with her cheekbones more intense, smile warmer, understanding deeper.

Where was I? Oh, yes. Max and I were discussing the matter loud enough to drown out a passing jet, until said lust object separated us and extracted mutual apologies. Then sweetened the deal by offering me the apartment while they visit her family in Greece, provided I cat-sit something called Slinky.

So here I am.

Seeing Ariadne again has opened up vistas of my past that I ache to investigate. Haven't felt so eager to write in years. Living here alone, undisturbed except by the people who deliver food, quietly except for the car alarms and Slinky's yowls, this has to open the floodgates.

Ezra to Dr. Fingerman: Lonely at the top
Seven days. Haven't left the apartment. Thousands of words written and thousands deleted. But, oh, the thoughts, Doctor Fingerman, the troubling thoughts!

What if Ariadne and I had gotten together back then.

What if I'd remained in NY after my play.

I should have followed my impulse to shoot the Times' critic, if only to save the world from the awful movies he has since directed.

Ariadne and me on a Greek island.

Max shooting me.

I keep the blinds closed against the world. Phones turned off and un-plugged. I'm growing a beard, unable to confront myself in the mirror. I suspect I pretty much stink. (Though it might be the cat box.)

What's your take on constipation? Is there a mental component or is it just nature's way of minimizing environmental pollution? I join Mozart in his gripe, "Another week and not a single movement completed."

My only amusement is exchanging emails with a hydra-headed corporation named Sunimitsu Heavy Industries that controls my mother's destiny.

Yet I feel oddly refreshed. This is the decompression I need before re-entering L.A. Even though Serena gave me the mission of separating my son from his bride-to-be and I wound up house-sitting for them instead.

Ezra to Sunimitsu Heavy Industries: Total incompetence
Once again I have a delusional notice from you whining that you have not received this month's payment for the room in your Silver Gables Retirement Residence occupied by my mother, Occupant #86520-Q.

Attached is my canceled check, enlarged for easy reading by your myopic & cataract-ridden eyes.

Congratulations on your increased efficiency. Normally you send me this notice every five or six months, but this time you waited only three.

P.S. Credit me $325 for the time I spent retrieving this check from my bank's electronic storehouse. Plus 5% for consumables.

Sunimitsu Heavy Industries to Ezra Popkin: Occupant #86520-Q

Thank you for bringing this error to our attention. It has been credited per your request.

You will soon receive a coupon book for convenience in keeping monthly payments current on your new Sunimitsu Heavy Industries Special Edition Motor Home.

Welcome also to the Sunny Open Roaders Club. Your six-month free membership entitles you and your loved ones to a 10% discount at Sunimitsu Heavy Industries Resort Hotels and subscriptions to all Sunimitsu Heavy Industries Media Division publications.

"A single hubcap may reflect the
full moon and all the stars."
Masaru Kuriama,
Founder & President, Sunimitsu Heavy Industries.

Ezra to Hotel Aegean guest Ariadne Koppos: a heads-up

A pair of Neanderthals entered your apartment at 7AM two days ago with a pass key. They muttered something incomprehensible to a barely awake me as I stumbled out of the bedroom. Then they proceeded to attack the bathroom walls with jackhammers. I asked them to leave. They refused. The argument escalated. Then a second crew trampled in with the intention of removing the living room windows.

Whether I became a raving lunatic who threatened one of them with his own pipe wrench (as Mrs. Epstein, your neighbor across the hall, insists) or simply scared the bejeesus out of the jackhammer brigade with my righteous indignation (my view), they finally cleared out.

Not only from your apartment, but from the entire building. I learned later it was about to be retrofitted with insulated windows and copper plumbing. The workmen refuse to return until there are no crazies around to threaten their lives.

Your Tenants' Committee is as vicious a collection of righteous loudmouths as I have ever run into this side of a producer's office.

When not threatening me with physical violence, they slip letters under the door promising lawsuits.

I'm sure this will blow over by the time you're back, but wanted you to know why you might be receiving a few glares. Sorry for the over-reaction. I have a tragic history in the remodeling department.

Max to Ezra: That's it!
I intercepted your typically self-centered email to Ariadne. This is the last straw.

I've been inventing excuses all my life for your total lack of concern about anybody except yourself: you were creative and I wasn't, I ought to be grateful you left me alone to discover who I was, etc.

Bullshit. You are a controlling egocentric monster. Your attempt to bully me into giving up the woman I love made me see you so clearly, and more important to see myself.

Actually, I owe you big time for that. I've been struggling with a dif-ficult decision and you helped me finally make the right choice. Ariadne needs a kidney transplant. I'm donating one of mine. Your example made me realize how awful it is to live selfishly.

Don't be there when we come back. Tell Mrs. Glick in 10D, directly above. She'll feed Slinky.

Ezra to Max: Kidney?
Please tell me you're indulging in the family sin of hyperbole. Max, the truth. Because if you're trying to shock me, you have.

Re the above Mrs. Glick, she starts clog dancing every midnight for hours, her contribution to the tenants' ugly war against me.

Max to Ezra: Good
Why do you find it surprising that I'd donate an organ to someone I love? Wait, I know: Because altruism is not in your vocabulary.

Mrs. Glick was a prima ballerina with the Ballet Russe de Monte Carlo. Clog dancing is pretty admirable at her age. Leave and you won't hear it.

Ezra to Max: More details
About the kidney, not Mrs. Glick, who will now haunt my nightmares in a tutu.

I'm concerned, Max. Come on.

Max to Ezra: Details

The timing is up to Ariadne and her doctor. She had a transplant in her teens. She might get another six months out of it. We're trying to hold off until the restaurant is up and running.

Donation is a routine procedure, I'll be good as new in a week.

Thanks for your late-blooming fatherly concern.

Ezra to Max: Routine my ass

Major surgery ain't chopped liver (at least not intentionally). It's a goddamn scary business. I've written enough operations to know.

Next time Ariadne's doctor passes off organ transplant as "routine," ask why the check he/she writes for malpractice insurance equals the national debt of Paraguay.

Hard to believe, but I was once your age, with the same future-be-damned passion for someone. When "forever" came up short we only had to divide books and records. It's gonna be real tough asking for your kidney back.

Not a joke, Max. Think.

Serena to Ezra: What have you done?

Max called from Greece to announce he's donating a kidney to this woman and claims you persuaded him to do it. True?

My head is spinning, Ezra. First you tell Max to seek out an ancient love-object of yours, then you encourage him to be her personal organ bank. Are you out of your mind?

Stay there. When they return have another talk with him. Talk to her. I'd be there myself if I weren't up to my ears with the most exciting work I've ever done. (A rumor going around that I'm short-listed for a Genius Grant. Does this sound totally crazy to you?)

Ezra to Dr. Fingerman: Patricide

Max is gifting his fiancée with one of his kidneys (rings are so last year). He claims I helped him reach that decision and is therefore firing me as his father. No, I don't understand either but there it is.

Maybe he just doesn't need a father anymore, now that he's doubling up on mothers.

Who should I approach first, Max or her? What's persuasive? Please respond ASAP.

Dr. Fingerman to Ezra: Reevaluation

I can no longer pretend to be of help.

After four decades of believing myself a successful healer you have forced me to see that most people, if given a second chance at happiness, would bungle that as well. The past has nothing to teach us, the future is inevitably repetition.

One has wasted so many years. All quite unsettling. I feel poised on the brink.

Ezra to Dr. Fingerman: Unacceptable

No quitting, not while I'm trapped in this apartment, despised within the building and on the streets outside, including the kids who deliver take-out. (I eat nothing until the cat tastes it first. And after the Thai pepper incident, Slinky isn't terribly fond of me, either.)

I spend sleepless nights before the TV, absently clawing at my face, yearning to run naked through the streets screaming, "Mea culpa, mea Max culpa!"

Restrained only by the residents' committee celebrating Walpurgisnacht outside my door.

Overhead, tutued Mrs. Glick clog-dances at midnight.

While my wife has assigned me the job of Mr. Fixit, for which I am no better suited than Genial B&B Host. When did I lose control of my life?

So you are poised on some imagined brink does not cut the mustard, Dr. Fingerman. Tell yourself, "This is not an end, it is a beginning." As I did at 3AM while poised on my own very real window ledge.

All I ask is a hint of a way out. Surely you can provide that. If only by rote.

P.S. What's your favorite sleeping pill these days? Various meds in the bathroom cabinet here must all be placebos, utterly ineffective though I chuck them down like M&Ms.

Dr. Fingerman to Ezra: Forgive me
Thank you for not allowing me to give in to despair. I am rereading notes of gratitude from former patients to buoy my spirits.

For your part, don't be so harsh on yourself. Try not to dwell on your many failures as a playwright, father, writing partner husband, son, etc.

For example, your attempt to murder your partner, however brutal, need not have destroyed that relationship. After spending some time in his company, I believe Stanley to be a kind, decent and forgiving man.

Ezra to Dr. Fingerman: Time in his company?!!
You are not allowed to have a relationship with my ex-partner. It is beyond unethical, it is incestuous.

Henry Lifshultz, Heating & Air Conditioning to Ezra: A real bargain
Remember me who received your thrilling movie by mistake? You mentioned needing an office. Still?

A few years ago my accountant (may his calculator explode in his face) put me into a nine-unit mini-mall. He swears the cash flow from these things is unbelievable. You rent to a dry cleaner, a nail salon, an Indian restaurant, all the usual hard-working immigrants, they'll support you in your old age.

Today his story is: How could he know tenants wouldn't stay because there aren't enough parking spaces?

This morning I woke up thinking, how much parking can a writer like you need? A movie script doesn't depend on walk-ins or even a classy window display. Your agent does all the work, right? And how often would your agent drop in, once a week? Frees up a lot of parking for my other tenants.

So I can offer you a terrific deal on store-front office space in the heart of Sherman Oaks, and will throw in mini-blinds for the windows if you like privacy. You want a sign with your name on it? That too.

It's available first of the month. Attached is a data sheet with lease terms, square feet, address, etc. Maybe someday I'll put up a plaque saying this is where you wrote your Oscar movie.

Sincerely yours, Henry Lifshultz

Ezra to Henry Lifshultz: Done!
You have the best timing since Johnny Carson. I am honored to become your tenant, site unseen. Suddenly I believe, as I have not for many months, that the future does, indeed, lie ahead.

Forgive me if I ramble, but claustrophobia and sleep deprivation (unrelieved by a tasty confection of other people's pills) do cloud the thought process.

A sign of one's own! I've always wanted my name up in lights. Can I have a sign that blinks off and on?

Won't be in L.A. for a week or so. Must await the return of my son and Melina Mercouri, his not-so child bride, in order to finalize their alienation. I'm only following orders. How wrong can that be? Hold it. My twanging synapses feel like...they might just, finally, be flipping me...ah, yes...into dreamland.

There is a goggg

Home from Greece, Ariadne unlocks her seventeen locks and enters the apartment, where there is darkness at noon. She finds Ezra lying mind-clogged on the living room floor, trying to project laser beams from his eyes up into the Glick apartment.

Slinky the cat sits on his chest planning the best way to smother him the next time he dozes off.

"Hello?" Ariadne inquires. "Max said you wouldn't be here, that you had to leave town suddenly."

"Where is he?"

"Business at the restaurant. He's coming. Why is your hand bandaged? Is that blood?"

"Oh, few scratches from trying to feed Slinky."

Her glance takes in the mess—empty food containers, strewn newspapers, crumpled Kleenexes, scattered books from her bookcase that Ezra briefly tried to read and tossed over his shoulder.

Ariadne opens the blinds. Sunlight floods in. She begins methodically to clean up.

As casually as one can speak such words, Ezra says, "So. I hear Max is giving you one of his kidneys."

"You think I'm taking advantage of him."

"Never said that."

"Then you approve. Not many fathers would."

He's thrown by how easily she flipped him. At that moment he should have realized his neurons are not firing on all cylinders, that disaster lurks around the corner if he keeps talking.

"I don't approve. But it's his kidney. How urgent is it, anyway?"

"Max insists on donating. Six months or so."

"Any chance getting married is only his idea?"

"Pretty much. I already tried married."

"What happens if he changes his mind about donating?"

"I go on a list. I look up relatives. We're a close family. Right now I bear in my body the last living part of my Uncle Nikodemos. I've tried to give him a good and fulfilling second life." She taps herself just above her left buttock. "You hear me, Uncle Nik? Have I not treated you okay?"

Ezra hears a voice incredibly like his own cry out, "Take my kidney, please!" Why is it saying this?

She stares at him for a long time. "Are you on something?"

"My kidney has more experience than Max's. You'll be happier together."

"Max would hate you."

"Say it was a newly discovered relative."

"He's right. You're a manipulator."

"Did he mention how inept I am at it?"

She seems to find that charming.

Now he hears himself saying, "Look, you don't know how long this thing with Max will last. On the other hand, with me you already have nothing. Isn't that simpler?"

"I'll think about it."

"Only rational people think. Come on, what's a kidney or two between friends?"

"We may not be compatible, like me and my kids. What's your blood type?"

"Same as Max's. Did you honestly find my play incomprehensible? It wasn't meant to be read, you know, it was a stage piece."

"You lost me after 'Act One: Inchoate Chaos Dissolves into

Nothingness.'"

"You remember that?"

"Weirdly. Are you sure you want to do this?"

"Positive."

"I'll think about it."

"It's the right thing. We both know that."

"Maybe I do like you."

Both parties are shocked to hear Max announce, "I despise you."

They turn to him with the same mental question: *How much have you heard?*

Max says, "You're supposed to be gone." And to Ariadne, "How can you like him after all you know?"

Two sighs of relief.

"Max, I was thanking your dad for taking such good care of Slinky."

"A prince among cats," Ezra says. "Actually saved my life once. Well, I'll take a minute to pack, then mosey on. Y'all keep in touch, y'hear? I mean it. Every word." The last aimed meaningfully at Ariadne.

Ezra to Serena: Homeward the hero

My mission was a brilliant success. Max's kidneys are safe where they are. Won't bore you with details. He doesn't yet know he didn't make the cut, so mum's the word if you speak to him.

Also, their marriage is unlikely. That's just Max's fantasy, and Ariadne's too kind to puncture it. We do have her to thank for his new career. So let's not think unkindly of Ariadne. We owe her. Let's remember that.

I'm finally on my way to visit mom for a few days. Then home, where I've leased an office in Sherman Oaks. All will be different from now on. I have learned the art of acceptance.

Ezra to Ethel Popkin, Silver Gables: Better late

Dear Mom,

Sorry about being out of touch for weeks after promising to show up the next day. No, I didn't have an accident, but I was wearing clean underwear anyway.

Actually, I did have an accident at the professional level, forcing me to spend time in Stockbridge buried in legal stuff. Then a few days at Max's place in NY.

But I'll definitely be in Boston this afternoon, word of honor, and will make up for disappointing you. Like a special dinner tonight, okay?

Love, Ezzie

Ethel, Popkin Silver Gables to Ezra: From your mom
Dear Ezzie,

I don't think I can see you. Lester is already taking me out to dinner tonight and then to a concert at Symphony Hall. Do you realize in all my years in Boston I never went there?

We're spending tomorrow together, too. We're riding the swan boats and then going to a baseball game. Do you remember when daddy took you on a swan boat and you cried because the man wouldn't let you pedal it yourself?

Life is so full of surprises. Just when you think there are none left worth waiting for. I hope you don't still hate swans. Maybe you can visit another time.

Your loving mother, Mom

Ezra to Minerva, Silver Gables: Lester?
My mother claims to be painting the town red with someone named "Lester." Is he a real person?

Minerva, Silver Gables, to Ezra: Racism
You wrote your mom you wouldn't take her to your old neighborhood where you grew up because it's dangerous now. Remember, that was when you were coming the next day and still aren't here?

Well, I happen to live in your "old neighborhood," and it is a fine community. I don't know what gives you the right to think your kind of ghetto, like it was then, is better than our kind of ghetto.

I took your mom to visit there myself after she waited all day for you to show up. We went to the apartment you used to live in, currently occupied by Mr. Lester Hemmings, a retired gentleman who recently lost his wife with a post office pension.

Mr. Hemmings showed your mom around the place. She remembered where every stick of furniture used to be when she lived there but said he certainly made it feel comfortable. Soon they were getting along like they knew each other forever, talking about everything under the sun.

Including children disrespecting parents who sacrificed to bring them up.

I don't know where your racism comes from, but certainly not from your lovely mother.

Ezra to Minerva, Silver Gables: Rosa Parks Scholarship Fund
Sincere apologies for my inadvertent racism. I've sent a healthy contribution to the above-named worthy cause.

Tell mom I'll be there about five today and hope she can fit me in.

Ethel Popkin to Ezra: Your surprise visit
Dear Ezzie,

It was so exciting that you were finally able to visit.

Doesn't Lester's son have a lovely home? Hope you had fun at the barbecue. Was your asthma bothering you? Lester's son said you seemed to have trouble breathing while he was telling you how much went wrong with his new kidney-shaped pool because today nobody gets anything right the first time.

Isn't Lester the sweetest, kindest man? Don't believe for one minute I'll ever forget daddy but life goes on and like they say think of the alterations.

Lester "googled" Serena for me. She's so famous! You must be proud of her, able to think up all those houses! But I bet she doesn't fly in private jets like you do. Give her my love.

Hope you had a safe trip back to Los Angeles.

Your loving mother

Ezra to Dr. Fingerman: Los Angeles bound
Am now departing Boston, where my mother has become twenty years younger and I am on the NAACP's most-wanted list

Do I risk telling my wife about Magda and clear the air? What about my impending kidney donation? Will telling her about that help or hurt?

I was just trying to sell a goddamn screenplay. Did Alfred Hitchcock have to go through all this?

Dr. Fingerman to Ezra: Insights
Is your offer of a kidney a surrogate for forbidden desires, i.e. a guilt-free way to enter Ariadne?

A thought experiment: Imagine yourself speaking to your kidney as Ariadne spoke to hers. What would you inquire of it, confide to it?

Ezra to Dr. Fingerman: For this I kept you from the brink?
The first thing I'd ask my kidney is Why do I continue with a therapist who's become as loony as I am?

And my kidney will reply, "Because you have no place else to go. Now piss off. Right now. I mean it, literally, hurry, please."

So excuse me, Dr. Fingerman, I have to find the men's room. (I'm at Logan waiting for my L.A. flight.)

Okay. Back.

Couldn't you have suggested a more relevant question? Like when my time comes to donate, how do I explain to Serena that big, ugly scar I came home with?

Just writing that last sentence makes me queasy. Have I mentioned that I faint at flu shots?

How the hell do I get out of this? I mean without having Ariadne rip the medals off my chest, slash my epaulets and spit on my shoes. I could not bear that. Oops, my plane's boarding. Despite everything, home has never looked so good.

Ezra to Serena: Hell & Damnation
WHY IS OUR HOUSE RAISED TEN FEET UP ON STILTS?! Burglar-proofing, improve the view? Goddamn it, you've gone too far!

I come home from LAX exhausted, schlepping my bags like Willy Loman, desperate for a drink and a flop. Except our front door is unreachable. How in hell am I supposed to get up there? My Swiss Army Knife doesn't happen to be the model with the ten-foot ladder.

If I wanted to live on stilts I would join the circus. Why don't you answer your phone? Where are you?

• • •

Serena to Ezra: Welcome back
House is elevated so I can slip in a new first story underneath. Cheaper than adding second story above former first story (No new roof, etc.)

Shlomo should have left a ladder. See if it's behind the garage. If not, splurge on the Presidential Suite at the Sportsman's Lodge.

Don't blame you for being furious. But this experiment has paid off big time. A potential client I desperately wanted saw the temporary stilts, thought they were my final design for a "castle in the air" look and fell in love with my creativity.

Picked me to create his dream house on a hilltop in the Hollywood Hills using the same concept. Endless budget. Our cash flow will be ok for some time.

Based on a few meetings so far, he'll be a joy to work with. A risk taker. Imaginative. Creatively simpatico. This project really has me excited.

I'm at U.C. Berkeley today, guest lecturer at school of architecture. Back tomorrow PM. Congratulations on resolving the situation with Max.

Welcome home. Love.

Ezra to Dr. Fingerman: Paging Dr. Richter
It's three AM. Woke up rigid with terror. A heavy wind is making my entire house sway under me because it's elevated on skinny stilts. I had to shlep a twelve-foot ladder from behind the garage to climb up into it. Would a sane person erect a house on stilts in earthquake country? Can we have my wife put away? She is a danger to herself and others.

She did it, Doctor, Serena did this to me. I try to remember when our marriage reached the tipping point that would permit such callousness. When her income became equal to mine? When mine began to shrink and she kept going? (Income, Doctor, goddammit, income!)

Dr. Fingerman to Ezra: Stilts? Rigid? Erect?
Your words suggest a deep angst about waning manhood, perhaps your fear that this recent sexual extravaganza may have been a final guttering of the candle.

I, too, feel the twilight of potency.

Lately I am compelled to write letters to patients of many years past, seeking forgiveness for failing them. I lack the courage to mail these notes (and the financial resources for lawsuits sure to follow). Yet I compose them one after the other, often long into the night. As I was when your email arrived.

The next morning Ezra sets out to climb down to retrieve his newspaper from the rubble that used to be his driveway, only to discover the ladder lying flat on the ground. Alarmed at being trapped aloft, he phones Shlomo, to demand his immediate appearance. By the time the contractor's pickup arrives two hours later Ezra is pacing like a tiger in a birdcage.

Shlomo resets the ladder more securely.

"There, all nice and solid for you," he shouts up to hyper-ventilating Ezra. "You have to remember, with ladders it's not just where the bottom goes, the top is also important."

"Thanks. I'll inscribe that in my Book of Memories."

"Invest in a good pair of rubber-soled shoes. You'll be using this for a while."

"Be more specific."

"Deck shoes."

"How long, Shlomo?"

"Frankly? This project's dead in the water until we fix code violations with the Building Department." He adds mournfully, "A slow process. Hardly anybody takes bribes."

Shlomo shakes his head as if that were a perverse form of corruption designed to make life harder for the working man.

"Even then," he goes on, "who knows when she'll come back to finish this? Now Xanadu is the most important thing in her life. That's what the new client calls his dream house. Xanadu. Yes, sir, Ezra, I'd buy deck shoes. Maybe two pair."

Shlomo leaves shaking his head, whether in despair or amusement Ezra cannot tell. He has no doubt about his own seething state of mind.

Late that afternoon Serena phones from Berkeley to suggest they meet for dinner this evening to celebrate his return. She names a restaurant they rarely visit because only Ezra favors it. Would eight be okay? She'll come straight from LAX.

Ezra is waiting at the restaurant's bar half a hour early. Something about this is setting off alarms. Why here? A year ago they argued over whether the food was barely edible (her) or great checkered-tablecloth Italian; whether the noise level was like the pleasant hubbub of a small town piazza (him) or just too damn loud.

Then there's the matter of her welcoming him home at all, a highly uncharacteristic move these days. What is he being set up for? Does she know about Stockbridge? Could there have been a spiteful email from Magda who's still stewing over his lack of B&B commitment?

He looks around. Is this the sort of restaurant Serena would choose to eviscerate him in? Her sense of high style might consider it ironically appropriate. Then he spots his wife entering. She has a big smile for him. Ezra relaxes, chiding himself for the guilty contortions he's twisted himself into. She's the one who put up those fucking stilts!

At their table over pre-dinner drinks Serena says she can't blame him being upset about the condition of the house.

"Condition of the house? You make it sound like someone forgot to dust."

"Okay. Maybe I went too far. Although considering the client it snagged—"

"You enjoy using that damned ladder to come and go?"

"Been doing it for a week, Ez. Lot cheaper than the gym. Might be good for us. Stop rolling your eyes."

"Sudden changes in elevation do that."

"Okay, I promise, no more design surprises."

"I appreciate the sentiment, but history is against you."

"I mean it. Word of honor."

"You lost your honor a long time ago."

"Second chance?"

Why is she so goddamn cordial? Well, he's in no mood to tolerate wifely kindness, not this husband just back from frolicking with a sex-charged member of the bar.

"You have enough stress in your life without my adding to it," Serena is saying as Ezra tries to erase "sex-charged member" from his mental loop.

Is her concern feigned? A trap? Does she know more than she's letting on? Although maybe her warmth is real. Either way this could be prime time for confessing all, as part of him desperately needs to. To explain that the mind-blowing fiasco with P transformed him into a hollow shell, an automaton who cannot be morally responsible for subsequent choices no matter how vile.

Later actions in New York would reinforce his case. Donating his own kidney, for god's sake? Even if, looking back, he recalls that in making the substitute offer to Ariadne he felt a rare flush of love for his son.

Serena would understand that part. He can at least tell her the truth about the kidney. Yes. Soon.

"So. Now that you're back" she says, "any replacements on the horizon?"

Ezra flinches, almost knocking a dish of risotto from the server's hand. "Beg pardon?"

"A replacement for Stanley. Any ideas about a new partner?"

"Not looking. Plan to write solo." To her raised eyebrows he adds, "Not one word."

"That's what I'm afraid of."

"Dammit, Serena."

"Sorry, slipped out. Of course it's your choice totally."

"Well. Thank you."

"I mean I'd be a hypocrite if I didn't agree that each of us is the best judge of her own career decisions."

"And life decisions," Ezra adds firmly. He swigs more wine and hurls himself into his risotto.

"Did you go down on someone?"

"What?"

"Are you coming down with something? You look sickish."

"You're right," he says, "this place is too noisy."

After dinner they drive home in silence. Unsure of ladder-climbing protocol, Ezra gallantly waves Serena ahead, then follows.

Halfway up he decides What the hell let's at least get the kidney on the table.

"What happened in Stockbridge, I mean the outrageous, stupid fraudulent—that is, you have to understand how it scrambled my emotions—then Stanley's fury—I mean, when your best friend turns on you—"

Ezra reinforces his agitated blurtings with wild gestures that unfortunately cause him to lose his grip on the ladder, and he falls off with a yelp, hitting the gravel hard.

When both Popkins finally climb into the house Serena sponges the blood away from his scraped elbow and covers the wound with a gauze pad and tape. Ezra trusts that his stoic silence during this painful procedure is all the "I told you so" necessary.

Next morning, with Serena off to work early and chipper, Ezra sinks onto the living room sofa to assess his current place in the universe. On the coffee table before him are bagel, coffee and computer. He discovers that the view through the temporary (hah!) wall of plastic sheeting is much improved by the elevation, not that he would ever admit it.

Ah, but of more immediate importance, the silence. No hammer blows, no whirs of saws, no air compressors, no Shlomo sounds at all.

Blessed silence. Well into the foreseeable future.

There arises in him a rebirth of hope. Live in the present. Finish the screenplay that faithless Stanley walked out on. Then write one alone. Yes. He can do that. Fuck them all.

An email interrupts. At first glance it seems to be from his therapist.

Not quite.

Bella Fingerman to Ezra: How dare you

I could tell you the names of movie people far more important than you think you are who owe everything to Dr. Sidney Fingerman. People who cried when he announced his retirement and begged him to stay on, who showered him with alligator luggage and autographed pictures.

But even these people with egos as big as the Ritz, they would never think for a second about disturbing Sidney's well earned retirement.

But not you Mr. Needy Writer! Thanks to you my Sidney is back in business whether his peace-of-mind likes it or not. After promising me we would spend more time together with maybe a cruise to Hawaii.

Worse, this brilliant healer who used to treat patients in an office furnished with expensive antiques and triple-ply Kleenex, he is reduced to practicing therapy from a filthy car that it never occurs to him to take to the car wash. He claims he works from his BMW 7 Series for patient privacy, because sometimes when he was emailing you in the house I looked over his shoulder if I was passing by and made suggestions. Who said he had to take them?

He barely sleeps anymore. He writes letters to former patients living and dead. He comes home with sawdust on his Cole Haan loafers that I gave him for his birthday, probably from some low class bar.

I will not allow you to destroy my Sidney. Leave him alone or I will do whatever it takes.

Ezra to Dr. Fingerman: Who she?
I have received a threatening email from one Bella Fingerman. Anyone you know?

No response. Ezra returns to the problem of that nuclear inspector's murder. Negligible inspiration. Soon shifts to emailing Stanley, requesting that despite their differences he would appreciate learning what Stanley knows about Bella Fingerman, wife of Stanley's new BFF Dr. Sidney.

Moments later the phone rings. "What?" Ezra demands.

"Stop trying to piss me off with crazy emails!" It is Stanley sounding pissed off. "I'm not mad at you anymore, okay? I don't like you, I don't hate you, I just want to forget you. My life has moved on to a happier place."

"Glad to hear it. What about Mrs. Fingerman?"

"Understand, this does not cancel the twelve hundred twenty-nine dollars you owe me for my ticket home from that crazy person in Stockbridge."

"It's in the mail. Has Doctor Fingerman ever mentioned his wife being slightly strange?"

"Who?"

"His wife."

"Whose wife?"

"My therapist's. Your buddy. And don't deny it. He comes home with sawdust on his Cole Haans."

"Stop with the non-sequiturs! I'm trying to let bygones be bygones here!"

"You deny knowing Dr. Sidney Fingerman?"

"The only Sid I know is this lonely old guy who struck up a conversation after my lecture. Then he started dropping by my shop, because people who work with their hands impress the hell out of him. I let him sweep up the sawdust. He gets a kick out it."

"That's him."

"Your therapist? My god, Ezra, you're in worse trouble than I thought."

"His wife, Stanley, tell me about his strange wife."

"He's not married."

"How do you know?"

"Guess he mentioned it."

"Are you sure?"

"Ezra, I don't follow the man home."

"Fuck."

"What?"

"Another dunning email from the morons who run my mother's place."

"Still?"

"We'll talk again."

"No we won't."

"If you have a minute, think about an ingenious way to bump off that safety inspector. Old times' sake?"

Sunimitsu Heavy Industries to Ezra Popkin:
File # 973562957.852
SECOND NOTICE. Current month's payment past due. Full payment must be received within 24 hours of above date to avoid eviction proceedings.

> *"The potter shapes the clay, but only*
> *the bean curd knows the emptiness within the pot."*
> *Masaru Kuriama, Founder & President, Sunimitsu Industries*

Ezra Popkin to Sunimitsu Heavy Industries: Pay attention!
You already have your goddamn check. As you will see on your previous email (appended) you maliciously applied it to a motor home lease. Fix this now.

Apply payment to File # 973562957.852.

Except around these parts she's known as "Mom." And we don't take kindly to mustache-twirling strangers who mutter threats about putting her onto the streets. You hear me, Sunimitsu Heavy Industries? Back off!

With murder now on his mind, Ezra is able to create a helpful back story for his stubbornly alive safety inspector: an Asian-American, he spent vacations in Japan helping his uncle run Sunimitsu Industries. There he and this senile relative (those ramblings at the end of Sunimitsu emails are the product of a failing mind) competed to see who could screw up the works faster.

Suddenly Ezra has dozens of possible demises bubbling in him. Only a matter of refining, selecting the most—

An email from his therapist interrupts:

Dr. Fingerman to Ezra: Bella Fingerman
Apologies for my mother contacting you. She has jealousy issues. The fault is mine. I promised that when I retired she would no longer have to share me with my patients.

We are working on it. I hope you will not allow mother's actions to affect our professional relationship.

Ezra to Dr. Fingerman: Au contraire, mon frere
This aspect of you is endearing. As someone who is also related to a mother, I appreciate the complications.

I assume that your mother does exist, and is not actually you in a wig , long dress and rocking chair. (Emailing at stoplights from your specially fitted BMW? The image tickles.)

Stanley tells me he and you are sweeping together. Better wipe the sawdust off your moccasins. Mother thinks you're frequenting low dives.

Ezra returns to murdering the safety inspector. Except an

email now appears whose sender's name triggers total brain freeze. He reads with numb fury.

Stefan Jibbet to Ezra: Old acquaintance be forgot

When I discovered who the architect of my Dream House was married to, I thought, goddamn, full circle, you can't make this stuff up. But hell, you must have no idea what I'm talking about.

I was that evil third-string critic who reviewed a play you probably don't even remember writing back in the Dark Ages. Who would've guessed I'd turn into an A-list director, and you'd become an industry legend by holding off Federal Marshals long enough to pitch a screenplay?

And now your wife brings us together again. God, irony is rampant in this town, isn't it?

If I may say so, that's one hot lady you're married to. And talented. Stilts! Damn! She's a female Brunelleschi. (Guy who did all those domes? Got a script on my desk about him. If it flies she's aboard as consultant.)

Our paths crossing again started me meditating on stuff like Time and the River. No matter how huge our current success, can it ever equal the wild joy of being poor, young and creative in New York? Man, I'd give my left Oscar to time-machine back for one day.

Love to finally meet you, rehash those great struggling-artist days. (My review water under the dam, right?) You like Café Fissionable? Best post-sous-vide food in town and every investor in the place has to be an Oscar winner. (I'm in for 10%. Aw, shucks.) How's lunch Wednesday?

Ezra speed-dials Serena's office, to be informed she is in a meeting and unavailable for several hours.

"I'll be there in fifteen minutes. Make her available!"

He starts out, then dashes back to send a quick email.

Ezra Popkin to Stefan Jibbet: Lunch impossible

You really don't want to sit across from me. I have this medical condition, a projectile vomit reflex in the presence of morons.

Events of the past are not, as you inventively phrase it, water under the dam.

Under the BRIDGE or over the dam, you literary, visual and cinematic buffoon.

Several near-accidents later Ezra marches into his wife's office. A half dozen architects are hard at work at their computers until he charges past them toward Serena's glass-walled conference room. He spots her with two employees studying plans and a model laid out on the large free-form table.

He throws the door open and aims a rigid finger at the end of a rigid arm at Serena.

"*J'accuse*, goddamit!"

Serena nods for the employees to leave. When the door closes behind them she says, "Sit down, Ezra. Please."

"Traitor! How could you?"

"Obviously you've learned about Stefan."

"Not from you, that's for sure."

"I intended to tell you last night. Can we all just sit down and let me explain?"

"You coupled insult with deception. Which would you like to explain first?"

"I wanted to tell you over dinner. But you seemed on the edge of hysteria. Later you fell off the ladder and that killed the rest of the evening. Ezra, please stop pacing. I intended to tell you!"

"Well, good old Stefan saved you the trouble. Barged right in with a fucking buddy-buddy email. Apparently he's in love with you."

"What?"

"Thinks you're the greatest thing since Brunelleschi. You know, the guy with the domes, unquote? How can you stand that pretentious shit?"

"Our relationship is professional. But I agree, at times he can be outrageous. Like you, Ezra. Just like you."

"Oh, no, you're not getting away with the old switcheroo. This is about you fulfilling the dream of the man who wrecked mine."

"This is about how I run my practice. Now dammit, sit, or this conversation is over." She indicates one of several skinny straight-backed objects around the table that she seems to consider chairs.

He lowers himself onto it with an insouciant defiance. It is more uncomfortable than it looks, painfully uncomfortable.

"Ezra, when the time came I moved on with my life. Stanley

moved on. Stefan moved on. Even Max has moved on. Only you remain fixated on the past, on that one moment when your hopes were crushed. I'm sorry, but I refuse to cater to that any longer."

Ezra stands, if only to relieve the discomfort.

Serena orders, "Sit down. Because now is the last time we will discuss this. Hear me out. Say what you have to. And then we'll be done with it. I said sit."

Ezra sits.

She continues, "You dare take offense at my choice of clients? After the many odious people from your business you've invited into our home, from coke sniffers to sniffers of under-wear? Yes, indeed. During one of our fourth of July barbecues I discovered a certain show runner, one of your pals, nosing his way through our laundry."

"Who? You never mentioned that."

"That's the difference between you and me."

"No," says Ezra, "the difference is that I put myself on the line solving real problems. In ways you can never imagine."

"Tell me."

"Irrelevant. I don't need my deeds memorialized in *Architectural Digest*."

"How about on a personalized license plate? The one you ordered when the Writers Guild gave a screenplay of yours honorable mention or something. You managed to squeeze that into six letters and numbers."

"Are you actually attacking my license plate? And what planet does this chair come from? Are their bodies radically different from ours? This thing sums up your ideas about how people are supposed to live in the world. Plastic sheeting for walls, our kitchen a doll's house version of Art's Deli, teetering stilts—"

"Don't lecture me about a world view, mister, not you with your bullying of Stanley, your stubborn insistence against all experience that you can survive without a partner, your total self-absorption…"

And so back and forth it goes for some time. Outside the glass wall Serena's employees watch entranced.

• • •

Ezra to Dr. Sidney Fingerman: Downward and backward
Send housewarming gifts. I've moved out of my house-on-a-stick into a
mini-mall. The American Dream full circle. Ancestors lived over the
store, I now live inside one.

Actually quite cozy. An inflatable mattress in the back room, a microwave, a magnificent espresso machine Stanley and I bought for our
office years ago and a twenty-four-hour opportunity to peek through
my blinds at the comings and goings of humanity in pursuit of Thai
massages, Indian food, dry cleaning, frozen yogurt, dry massages, Indian
cleaning, etc. To add insult to injury (my bloodied elbow throbs as I
type this), Serena is blithely designing a hilltop pleasure dome for a
critic who crapped on the best thing I ever wrote.

Or maybe worst thing. Distance lends disenchantment.

But this I do know. That play asked urgent, basic big-picture questions
that carried me into depths that were…well, way beyond my depth.
But it doesn't hurt to ask, does it? Which I did with a vengeance. And
of that, I am proud.

If I could only remember what all the fuss was about, what those
questions were. Nowadays my ontological musings boil down to this:
To kidney or not to kidney, that is the question.

My best to your mother. They say the Greek Isles are nice this time
of year.

Ezra to BunKumfi di Milano: Cruel & Unusual Punishment
Your company makes a so-called chair that I had the misfortune to
encounter in my wife's office yesterday.

Did you ever give this product a test run? Didn't anybody notice there
is no way in creation to be comfortable on it?

Perhaps its design was assigned by mistake to your Airplane Seat
Division, where the word "comfort" incites gales of laughter.

For whatever reason, half an hour with rump resting (hah!) on an
undersized triangular surface, back supported by a narrow slat with a
curve that contradicts my spine, that, sir or madam, is pure agony.

I would not have endured this for thirty seconds, were I not planted
there like a taffy apple on a stick, immobilized by a detailed lecture on
infantile self-destruction.

I beg you, recant your delusion that a chair must please only the eye and the tuchus can fend for itself. There is enough pain in the world already.

Stefan Jibbet to Ezra: Apologia
I sense your contempt for me. I have earned it.

What was I thinking back then? How could I imagine a review written by me—the guy your girlfriend was with before you—could ever be seen as anything but revenge?

Can you blame me, though? She was something, wasn't she? Admit it, if our positions had been reversed and you were the one she left because she wanted to be with me, you might've written the same vindictive hatchet job.

Okay, I went overboard. But remembering that play of yours today—from the perspective of the hard-nosed pros we've both become—can't we agree that it was mostly awful?

I mean, act one was, what, three hours long, ending with the destruction of the universe. Come on, what kind of story arc does that set up with seven more acts to go?

Some moments did impress me. Like when the actors ran up and down the aisles baring their asses and speaking in tongues—which, as I recall, were painted blue to match their asses.

Wonderful concept. At least when you're twenty. Like the program notes hand-lettered on pita bread. I remember, because about I AM the few audience still hanging in there began noshing on their programs.

Or who knows, maybe they were trying to satisfy a hunger deeper than hunger. You may have actually created a magical moment that transmogrified drama back into its religious roots.

(Nice turn of phrase, yes? Hey, you don't rewrite some of the best scribes in town without picking up a few tricks.)

An honest reviewer would have noted that coup de theatre.

But of course I wasn't honest, I was crazy pissed at the playwright jerk she left me for. So when the Times sent me out to a basement production of some play, I recognized your name and practically wrote my review going there on the subway.

Promise you, no matter how sleazy this incident makes me look, it stays in my upcoming memoir un-bleeped. (In hardcover and ebooks this fall—great gift for anyone in the biz.)

Still hope we can be friends. Know it'd please your beautiful wife.

P.S. Trying to remember the real name of Kelly Greenberg, that cute little wannabe actress we shared. Luanne? Was that it? Wonder what became of her. Hope she followed her bliss like we did.

Ezra glares at his computer, his past splitting open like rotten fruit. So Luanne came to his bed from the arms of the loathsome Jibbet—the latter's identity hidden from Ezra then and since.

On the other hand Luanne had no compunction about revealing Ezra's identity to Jibbet. The injustice rankles. What he and Luanne had back then surely demanded that names be named equally or not at all.

Bells jingle with the opening of his front door, interrupting dark thoughts about how thoughtless decisions forever skew the course of history.

A white-haired woman wearing a pink sweat suit peers in. "I need new soles on these shoes."

"Maybe next month." Ezra slams the bolt on the door after her and phones Morro Bay.

Luanne answers. "Hello?"

"Why didn't you tell me Jibbet had a reason to hate me?"

"Hi, Ezra. Little late for that discussion, isn't it?"

"Not according to him. Came right out with it. Even managed an almost human-sounding apology. How about that?"

"Well, I'm not surprised. Serena says he feels guilty about—"

"You know she's working with him?"

"We do talk. Oh, Ezra, last to find out?"

"Why didn't you tell me you had a history with Jibbet when his review came out? I might've read it differently, knowing he saw me as a rival not a playwright."

"To be honest, I was afraid you'd turn your rage onto me. Your mood those last days was really scary."

"Are you saying I was a monster? Is that how you remember our time? Me as a monster?"

"One who was out of control, apoplectic and two years old. Yes."

"How about before I was a monster? Not a word about Jibbet when we started out. But he sure knew my name. You think that was fair? Why the goddamn double standard?"

"Okay, then. This ring a bell?" She speaks with mocking theatricality. "Yesterdays no longer exist for us—the world begins anew with Lu 'n' me!"

Ezra groans at the memory. "Shit."

"Sure. But shit you proclaimed at parties, at bars, in bed and, on one giddy late night, in a crowded subway car. Always pointing out that you spoke genuine iambic pentameter. Well, I bought it, Ezra. Hook, line and no Stefan Jibbet. God we were young…god."

Ezra tries to decipher the sounds she is making. "Are you crying?"

"Nothing to do with you."

"Stanley?"

"He's changing. Nothing I can put my finger on. Incidentally, I told him about us."

"What?"

"We were arguing. I wanted to shock him. Okay, to hurt him."

"You throw this at him, about his wife and his best friend, and you wonder why he's changing?"

"He didn't know either one of us then."

"How'd he take it?"

"He laughed."

"Stanley laughed at us being together?"

"Uncontrollably."

"Why was that funny?"

"Ask him. All I know is he laughed and laughed until he started to gag and then he went out to make more furniture."

"That was it?"

"Subject hasn't come up since. Of course we don't talk much lately."

"When did you lay this on him?"

"About a month ago."

So Stanley knew during their Bella Fingerman phone call. Yet said nothing? Not for the first time, Ezra feels he lives in a world of secrets, puzzles and spiritual GPSs with blank screens. Others have keys, codes, passwords, only Ezra Popkin—

"Ezra, I'm sorry, it just came out."

"Forget about it. So. How did *you* like the play, Mrs. Lincoln? I mean, any chance you agreed with Jibbet's review?"

"Jesus, I was in the bloody thing, so I never got to see it, did I? Goodbye, Ezra."

"Wait—does Serena know?"

But Luanne has hung up.

•••

Stefan Jibbet to Ezra: Brilliant idea
Can't get that play of yours out of my mind. So going with my gut (never fails) I mentioned it to my dear friend Darcy Whippet, did my usual great selling job, making it sound totally quirky and gripping. Guess what? She thinks it could be perfect for a new multi-part thing she's producing.

Speed me a copy ASAP. If this goes, don't worry, I'll be looking over her shoulder all the way to protect you.

Has Serena shown you her preliminary designs for Xanadu? Wow! Curvy stilts sexier than stiletto heels! You are so goddamn lucky with marriage. Take it from a randy old triple ex.

Ezra to Stefan Jibbet: Go away
Your protecting me conjures up vision of being stuffed into a giant condom. You have the soul of a traffic cone. Leave me alone.

Ezra returns to his screenplay but is too upset to concentrate on story problems, so flees next door for early lunch at the Delhi Deli Indian restaurant where Mr. Ghupta serves extra-large portions to fellow tenants.

Excellent lamb tikka is restoring his will to live when Serena calls.

"How could you reject Stefan's offer like that?"

"I question his motives." Might this open the door to probing what she knows about Luanne and him, without tipping his hand?

"Just swallow your paranoia for once and hand over the play."

"We agreed not to interfere in each other's work. You made quite a point of it."

"This could be a game-changer for you, Ezra."

"Who in her right mind designs a house on stiletto heels? I mean, outside the flesh trade."

"They are not stiletto heels!"

"Your randy Xanadu Man disagrees. You do realize, this guy is leading you deep into kinkyville?"

Serena heaves an exasperated sigh. "Why do I bother?"

"Easy. We love each other. Just can't live in the same house. Maybe because it's like that Greek river, it's never the same house twice."

"You're a bulldog, Ezra, you refuse to let go. Should have known better. Sorry I interfered in your decision."

He is about to confess that the question of working with Stefan's buddy is moot because there is no extant copy of the play. But like Luanne before her, Serena abruptly hangs up on him. A pattern developing here?

Ezra to Dr. Fingerman: Hamlet of the Mini-Mall

Should I have accepted Jibbet's help with my career? I mean, ignoring that no copies of my play exist anymore, making that impossible. Yet the question nags at me. Would I become entangled with this pompous jackass if I could?

Back and forth I go. A hypothetical built on anti-matter. It does pass the time.

Interrupted by multiple daily visits to Yankel's Yogurt Land two stores down. Another notch in my belt. Outward bound.

Dr. Sidney Fingerman to Ezra: Your philosophizing

We both recognize avoidance when we see it, even if less harmful than avoidance techniques of other writers I have treated, i.e. adultery, shoplifting, self-mutilation, internet porn, drugs, alcohol. (Not a checklist).

Mother tells me she has sent you her home-made fudge brownies. Do not eat them. I refer, of course, to the impropriety of gifts from a member of my family to a patient.

Don't give the brownies to anyone else, either.

Ezra to Dr. Sidney Fingerman: Brownie points
Aha! So that's why I arrived at my storefront this morning to find a ring of dead rodents on the sidewalk around a gnawed-open Priority Mail package.

Are you sure I can't rewrap and forward to this director friend of mine?

"Did I predict a career bounce from your Bretton Woods meet, or did I not?" It's Brad calling from Talent Central. "You lucky bastard, I've snagged you a gig with Darcy Whippet. She of the many Emmys?

"No shit? You snagged her for me?" Ezra says with feigned awe.

"Lady's interested in a certain play you wrote, for an internet video series."

"A play of mine? Which one?" Ezra is enjoying this.

"Act One ends with the destruction of the universe, Act Two opens seven months later. Big cast, lots of locations. That's all Darcy knows, but she's panting over it. How fast can my guy pick up a copy?"

"Never, Brad. Never."

"Okay, I grant you she has a reputation as a ruthless, devious ball-buster. But since when are you in any position—"

"I'm in no position. But I know impossible."

"Look, Ezra, Stefan Jibbet recommended you to her, and you do not insult a friend of Jibbet's without consequences. Not to you—you were never going to work again anyway—but to me. How does it look if I can't even persuade someone like you to submit a project? What does that do for my credibility? You owe me, man. I kept you on long after you were dead meat."

"One maggot to another, hear this. No copies of that play exist anymore. None. Not a single page."

"You sure? I mean, maybe on some disk in your closet—"

"Long before disks. It's all been destroyed, Brad. Without a trace."

"I'm fucked."

"Well, if she likes my work, how about I pitch my headline story about nuclear energy—"

"Shut up, I'm thinking. We have to give her something on paper about that play. A quick outline. No, not enough. Reshape an unsold script. Yes. Top of your list here I see *Catman Duo*, your story about a French cat-burglar bigamist. Does it have to be Paris? Why can't it be the black hole at the end of the universe?"

Ezra to Dr. Sidney Fingerman: Crazy-making
A producer is lusting after my talent but only in the form of a play that no longer exists.

My agent is aware of this. Yet he expects me to deliver said play, since in this town non-existent properties regularly change hands for large sums.

When the play did exist I considered it trash because I believe everything I read in the New York Times.

I have since learned Jibbet's soul-crushing review was hogwash. Leaving me with my original suspicion that my play was a work of genius, which I can never confirm because all evidence has been deep-sixed.

Luanne, the only other witness, withholds her opinion, claiming she never actually saw the play, which I take as an indictment of it. Lately I take everything as an indictment. Besides that I eat too much yogurt.

I agree that little evidence of genius has shown up since then. But I'll take a flash in the pan over a poke in the eye any day.

Maybe Luanne kept a copy.

Luanne has not kept a copy, but she does remember they'd mailed one to his mother with one of the programs Luanne had lovingly hand-lettered on pita bread. Ezra's phone call to his mother is as unproductive as usual and no one else there will speak to him.

Ezra to Ethel Popkin: My play
Dear Mom,

You were right to hang up on me. I shouldn't have shouted at you. But I need to know if you still have the play I once sent you. Look where you keep my old report cards and clippings from early haircuts.

If you find it (the PLAY, please, not hair clippings) let me know right away. I'll have it picked up by FedEx. It will be okay to give it to them.

Can you look right now? Please?

Ethel Popkin to Ezra: Your wonderful play
Dear Ezzie,

Of course I still have your play. I take it out all the time to read what you wrote on the cover, Dedicated To The One Who Always Believed in Me. It's still in the same envelope you mailed it in including the program written on that big cookie. How clever!

I have often tried to read the rest but it's so heavy my arms get tired. I skipped to act 2, but that's even harder to understand. You really ought to make it easier when you reach act 2.

Daddy and I know how much you want to be famous. Try not to be too disappointed if this doesn't do it, remember you have a lot of time ahead of you and there's always a place where we don't care how often you fail.

Ethel Popkin surrenders the manuscript to the FedEx driver without incident, who over-nights it to Ezra, who hand-carries it to his agent, who messengers it to WhipDarce Productions.

Brad, Talent Central to Ezra: Rabbit out of hat
How in hell did you manage to put this together in two days, this cement block of a script you dropped off? (War & Peace backwards, in play format? Is there an app for that?)

Any case, your dedication to me on the title page was truly moving. The big cookie was also appreciated, but to be honest, the green frosting tasted a bit medicinal.

Darcy and I are still haggling over your money. Don't panic—it's already triple anything you've ever fetched before.

• • •

Darcy Whippet to Ezra: Glorious!
As Stefan promised, your exciting, wide-roaming play is the perfect vehicle to launch our groundbreaking new internet concept. Can you be here tomorrow at two? I have pages of notes for the adaptation.

Meanwhile, think about introducing a Stage Manager character, à la OUR TOWN, a sort of folksy Greek chorus who comments on what the other characters are thinking and feeling.

Ezra, be prepared to give this everything you have. Here at WhipDarce Productions we believe our innovative version of your script will become the new paradigm.

I so look forward to working with you. You're a very special talent.

At their inaugural meeting Darcy greets Ezra with a hug and kisses on both cheeks. He shakes hands all around with a half dozen excited people. Then all sit at the table with freshly minted copies of his play before them.

"I can't tell you how exhilarated I am. The grandness of your scope!" Darcy says. "The multiplicity and variety of characters, the endless locations!"

Attributes usually more toxic to producers than Bella Fingerman's brownies, a thought Ezra keeps to himself. "Yes. Well. You let the work take you where it wants to go."

"Where have you been? My god, listen to him! Thank you so much for coming here today, Ezra." She stands. Apparently that was it. "I wanted everyone to meet you personally as we launch this grand voyage of ours."

She hands him a thick folder of notes, tells him to let his magical imagination roam free, screw the budget and deliver a draft of segment one in three weeks.

Again kisses on both cheeks (In his state of suspended disbelief, Ezra half expects lower-cheek smacks as well.)

Back in his cozy storefront he prepares a cappuccino and ponders what it will be like to read his play for the first time in decades. He is wildly curious, faintly terrified.

He settles into his thrift shop overstuffed chair (how like that tatty wondrous chair of long ago!) and opens his manuscript to ACT ONE.

For the next hour he reads and reads and reads. And understands nothing. The thing is incomprehensible, each page more opaque than the one before. No part of it makes sense, not the plot, not the speeches, not even the page numbers. Even most of the words escape understanding—many of which he now recalls were his own invention (Young Ezra, the New Elizabethan).Yet Darcy gets it, Darcy loves it, Darcy expects segment one chop-chop.

With great curiosity he moves on to her notes, detailed suggestions about dialog, motivations, character development, story arc, the usual. Where is all this coming from?

Was his play deconstructed and then reassembled by non-English speakers? Is he the butt of a massive practical joke, Brad's comment about *War & Peace* backwards a friendly tipoff?

Yet his agent has informed him that a huge initial payment is already in his checking account, which his bank's web site now confirms.

Teeth gritted, headache persistent and gut churning, Ezra settles in for a long slog over post-apocalyptic ground. An unproductive Day One rolls over into an even more arid Day Two. He devotes Day Three to buying a new computer, after an unfortunate incident in late afternoon of Day Two.

Henry Lifshultz, Heating & Air Conditioning to Ezra: Drywall
Dear Mr. Popkin:

As your landlord I must ask you to refrain from further damage to my walls. Your next-door neighbor Mr. Ghupta was passing by when the incident occurred. You actually threw your computer?

I would imagine my enclosed bill for $247.93 to repair the drywall pales by comparison with replacing your computer, although the price of drywall goes up all the time while I see computers go down, so who knows.

Be assured, I understand the Artistic Temperament and make allowances.

Sincerely yours, Henry Lifshultz

Ezra to Dr. Fingerman: Stuck, oh
I have been mercilessly bribed to adapt my long-lost play for the internet. (Yes, I know the hazards of adapting the work of a living writer. One minor novelist whose book Stanley and I adapted—and improved—still calls me in the middle of the night years later, to mutter a drunken curse and hang up. If I start receiving angry calls from myself you'll be the first to know.)

Initially this play adaptation of mine presented a major difficulty, namely, that I found it incomprehensible.

As a result the total product of my labors until a couple of days ago was one laptop fatality, and one house call by Superior Drywall, Plaster & Stucco, No Job Too Small. (Whose plasterer made my day by commenting, "Ironic a writer should be my last job, now I'm signing a four-picture deal with Grand Lux Productions.")

To the casual passerby—say, a curry-pushing tattle-tale—it might appear that yet again I let panic trump creativity. Not so. In my blind thrashings I stumbled across a key to the crypt. To wit, the very notes that helpful Darcy overloads me with.

Using her suggestions , instructions and commentary, I work backward to tease out my original text. She is the Rosetta Stone by which I reconstruct my play. Call it reverse engineering.

So I charge ahead, stumbling and picking myself up and stumbling again. But the pages pile up. And thank god they do, because she calls daily for progress reports and regular meetings at her office.

No question I'll hit bumps along the road—already have, literally, an outbreak of hives on a site too embarrassing to scratch in public. (Are you under unusual stress lately, asked my doctor. My reply: a long nervous giggle worthy of Peter Lorre. Doc hastily scribbled an rx for a large economy size anti-anxiety med while backing out of the room.)

Dr. Sidney Fingerman to Ezra: Your moods
First great anxiety from pressure to sell a play that does not exist. Now great enthusiasm to adapt that play though it is incomprehensible.

Such mood swings worry me.

Ezra to Dr. Fingerman: My oil addiction
Cease, Dr. Macbeth, stop with the double, double, toil and trouble. All's well. I have learned to go with the flow, and I mean that literally.

Four words have transformed my life, and they can yours, too: Change Your Own Oil. Been practicing it for years, and thought nothing about it except the ego-boost of having one task in life I'm able to manage with dexterity and assurance. Then last week a transcendental bonus kicked in (to be exact, at 175,129 miles).

Picture me rolling under my car supine on my mechanic's creeper. I unscrew the plug. Oil gushes out as expected. But this time I cannot take my gaze off the satiny black flow, transfixed as gush narrows to a pencil-thin stream, until it finally emerges drop by reluctant drop, each ebony globule unique as a snowflake. (I swear.)

Time stops. Anxiety vanishes. Purge begets purge, and I am reborn, again gung-ho to bootstrap my way up through more pages.

Sadly, this epiphany is available only at 5000 mile intervals.

Your professional opinion. Do I have the seeds of a religion here?

Ezra to Stefan Jibbet: This is not easy
I misjudged you. Thanks for the gig. Darcy says hello.

Ezra to Dr. Sidney Fingerman: Better than oil
As a professional healer, you might be interested in my latest psychic breakthrough (Presumably you've already published a paper on my oily nirvanas.)

At 10AM last Tuesday a hyper-ventilating panic attack erupted me out of my office, yearning to breathe free. A quick frozen yogurt soothed not at all, merely went straight to my expanded gut to say hi to all the yogurts of previous days.

If ever a man needed an oil change! But my odometer demanded 1721 miles more, roughly two round trips to San Francisco. Tempting but impractical.

Sitting in my car, the braying of National Public Radio fraying my nerves, I glanced at my neighbor three stores down, Forever Joyous Thai Massage. A pair of women were exiting. They were happy. Their step was light. Women leaving Forever Joyous Thai Massage always looked happy.

Though a massage virgin, I marched resolutely in, to a shop full of hardworking Asian masseuses who glanced up at me, then returned to their labors.

I introduced myself to the older woman in charge as a fellow tenant. Thanks to our garrulous landlord she already knew much about me. Could I bring my Oscar to work some day? How sad that my crazy partner would post filthy pictures of me on the internet. Where could she find them?

She offered a professional discount after I assured her that, yes, her life story would definitely make an exciting movie that we must collaborate on one day soon.

My masseuse, Betsiross, was a tiny woman with surprisingly strong hands that really did the trick. You would not believe how many positions she managed to twist my body into over the next hour, how many ways there were to tweak my extremities. (I see the inside of your car windows steaming up, Doctor. No lewd inferences, please.)

Anxieties gone, I moon-walked back to my own storefront, able to produce a whole hour's worth of pages for Darcy, who has begun introducing a Bad Cop to the Good Cop routine in her incessant phone calls. Then back to Bestiross for another massage and another hour's productivity. Those miracle hands of hers do squeeze the pages out of me.

Pages that offer a peek into my lost youth. What a pompous, self-absorbed know-it-all I was. And yet somehow endearing.

To maintain creative flow Ezra starts brainstorming aloud about his project during his sessions with Betsiross. Her English seems limited to such phrases as "Hurt good for you!" and "Why men complain so much?", but every so often she responds with a thoughtful, "Hmmm."

To Ezra's surprise this rote interplay helps him resolve knotty story problems. He urges her to comment more often. And so they forge ahead, she loosening kinks physical and mental, he prattling on insofar as his contorted body can make coherent sounds.

However, yelping out plot twists amidst shrieks of pain does raise a few manicured eyebrows among the other massagees, all female. After one highly vocal session the owner delicately suggests that he might prefer to meet with Betsiross more privately.

"We're still talking massages, right?" Ezra says.

"Massages, sure massages! What kind of place you think this is?"

"Sorry. Didn't mean to—"

"You want something else? I refer you."

"No, just Betsiross doing what she's been doing."

"You bet. She go to you, anyplace you like, only thirty dollars extra."

It is arranged that Betsiross will make house calls to the back room of his office, where Ezra is now free to give unbridled expression to both his pain and his thoughts. Productivity goes way up.

Especially since he has discovered that he can type notes and script changes into his laptop during massages, provided Betsiross is dealing with his lower half and the rest of him is minimally contorted.

"So in the context of the period in New York," he says, face down on the mat as she kneads his leg, "I must have meant—yieee!"

"Hmmm."

"Right, Stanley, maybe not."

A week later Ezra has a modus operandi that nicely balances massage (down to one every other day) with output (Darcy's Bad Cop is in retreat).

One afternoon he spots Ariadne's name at the top of an incoming email and his hard-earned equanimity comes crashing down. Transplant time? He opens the email with trembling finger.

Ariadne Koppos to Ezra: Your son
Have you heard from Max? We argued again about getting married—he can't accept it won't happen—and he moved out, which I suppose was inevitable. Also he missed an important appointment yesterday with the CIA .

I'm worried.

Ezra to Ariadne Koppos: Our Max
I wouldn't worry too much. He does this kind of thing. He'll reappear sooner or later.

Unless you mean he's running from the Feds. What's with the CIA? Some demonstration again?

Trust this finds you in good health.

Ariadne Koppos to Ezra: Max
It's the other CIA, an application interview with the Culinary Institute of America. Max is eager for professional training.

I think of you often, and worry about you, too.

Fondly,
A

Ariadne's emails overwhelm him, sting his chest like heartburn. He inadvertently hangs up on Darcy, deletes a day's total product, forgets how to touch-type.

He drafts a dozen emails to Ariadne trying to weasel out of his kidney offer. Deletes the lot. There wasn't one he'd care to find chiseled on his tombstone.

His script output drops to nothing. He requests an emergency massage from Betsiross.

"No time, Mr. Ezra, not until end of week, I am so busy."

It seems her business is booming. A quick study, Betsiross has been using her "hmmmm" response with other customers, who can't get enough of this deeply sympathetic listener.

"I think Babafrichee have time."

No thank you. Babafrichee lacks the touch and is too fond of garlic. (Who's naming these women, the DAR?) He emails a nine-one-one to Dr. Fingerman, but the good doctor sends regrets, too busy Netflixing *Citizen Kane* for that evening's cinema class.

Ezra tries a therapeutic spin in his car, which only aggravates his ramping sense of doom. Back at the mini-mall he parks in front of his storefront. The odometer indicates no oil change for another 842 miles. The hell with it, what price mental health? He needs his oil changed, and he needs it now.

He retrieves an oil filter and five quarts from his stash and jacks up the car's front end with his long-handled professional-grade hydraulic jack. He slides under the engine, supine aboard a four-wheeled mechanic's creeper. (Great for creeping under cars but a poor substitute for a skateboard, as he discovered in a test that left palms and knees shredded.)

Ten minutes later Ezra starts to relax, sheltered from the world by the mass of automobile suspended over him, mesmerized by the final drops dripping from the crankcase with such insouciance.

A sudden sound like the hiss of a snake shatters his repose—the jack is releasing! The engine jolts down to within an inch of his face, then roars to life. Tires squeal as the car backs out like a shot and races down the street.

Ezra can only lie there, immobilized by terror, gaping up at blue sky where once his car had been. Shoppers and store-owners rush to him. His neighbor from Superior Dry Cleaners helps him to his feet, then recoils.

"Some professional advice," the dry cleaner says, "Don't even think about trying to clean those pants."

The police find Ezra's car blocking traffic on Ventura Boulevard a quarter mile from the mini-mall, as far as the engine could make it without oil. A white man, perhaps black, maybe Hispanic, was seen sprinting away.

Ezra's nerves twang like country music the rest of the day. Betsiross cancels her last client to provide a free extreme massage, but her kindly infliction of pain still leaves him a bundle of nerves.

Bedtime, and no relief despite a dinner of donated lamb tikka washed down by three vodka tonics. He locks the door, switches off the lights and retires to his inflatable mattress in the back of the shop. He relives his under-car horror before at last sleep overwhelms him.

He dreams of botched organ transplants and poison cookies, until he's jolted awake at 1AM by the sound of his front door opening. Mother Fingerman coming after him in person?

He recalls warnings about a rash of break-ins at mini-malls. He fumbles in the dark for his cell phone and whispers to 911 for help, even as the curtains part that separate his sleeping quarters from the front of the shop.

A figure enters with a dim flashlight and immediately bumps into the table holding Ezra's huge brass and nickel-plated espresso machine. There is a crash and a cry.

(Ezra and Stanley bought the machine for their office as a consolation prize. What they actually wanted was to invest in a coffee shop franchise, which Luanne put the kibosh on. "It's a fad," she said, in words that still echo in Ezra's nightmares, "I mean, how long will people pay five dollars for coffee with funny names like 'latte' and 'cappuccino'?")

Ezra tries to escape but stumbles over the fallen intruder. They tussle until Ezra breaks free, only to be staggered by a blast of pepper spray.

The police arrive (second visit in twenty-four hours!) to find both Ezra and intruder weeping helplessly.

"Of course I let myself in," says the owner of Lifshultz Heating & Air Conditioning, blotting up tears. "It's a landlord's right to inspect the premises."

"In the middle of the night?" says an equally teary Ezra.

"My weekly poker game goes late because everybody's too old to sleep anyway. On the way home I decide to check on the current state of my walls in your unit. Do you blame me?"

"You could've knocked."

"Who knew you were living here full time? I can't find the light switch, so I stumble over the table and fall, with that fancy coffee thing of yours crashing down inches from my head. Believe me, a closer call than my Purple Heart from Korea."

"So then you used your pepper spray," says a weary cop who obviously wants the whole thing to be over. "In the dark. In every direction."

"How did I know my attacker was only this talented screenwriter? Even if he does have a history of aggression."

"I did not attack Stanley!"

Two days later Ezra learns that his car's engine melted like a Salvador Dali watch and then cooled into a nice anchor for someone's yacht, to the tune of $7957.23. Plus 5%. His insurance company is amused by his mechanic's estimate.

There is also an unusual post-traumatic-stress symptom.

Ezra to Dr. Sidney Fingerman: My autophobia

A botched car theft has left me traumatized. Namely, can no longer drive, as the sound of a car's engine starting up triggers sweating, trembling, a full panic attack. Discovered this when I turned the key in a rental car and my vigorous shaking set off the airbag.

I exaggerate, though only a bit. (But a warning light did come on: SEEK HELP IMMEDIATELY.) Will the symptoms fade? How fast? I'm forced to get around on a bicycle with a wobbly wheel, exchanged via craigslist for a broken espresso machine.

Dr. Pavlov, I don't have time for post-traumatic stress. Darcy demands a steady flow of pages.

Dr. Sidney Fingerman to Ezra: Your car theft

Why did you steal the car? Your symptoms' duration may depend on your motives. Was it a wild impulse during your manic phase?

Magnanimous Insurance Ltd to Ezra: Claim #5584bx

Engine replacement at cost of $7957.23 is denied.

Your policy does not cover loss due to improper maintenance. Our Claims Adjuster has determined that the engine failed because it was run without oil, contrary to instructions in your vehicle's Owner's Manual (page 93).

Ezra to Magnanimous Insurance Ltd: Claim #5584bx

I reject your rejection of my claim.

Despite the opinion of your claims adjuster (and the seeing-eye dog he rode in on) the destruction of my engine was caused by the thief who stole my car after I drained the oil—which I do like clockwork every 5000 miles. One Yuri Potemkin, service manager at my car dealership, will confirm that.

The cost of $7957.23 (plus 5%) is your responsibility, especially after the many multiples of that amount I have paid in premiums over the years. To say nothing of my future premiums, which you will doubtless triple to compensate for your hurt feelings.

Please send additional claim forms for mental impairment resulting from this incident.

"What horrible thing did you say to Max?" Serena demands on her first visit to her husband's mini-mall office. It is now a week after the car theft. Betsiross has been squeezing in extra mercy massages and Ezra has regained some of his momentum.

Serena enters as Ezra is on the phone arguing with his producer. Lately Darcy has been giving endlessly detailed notes about what the characters should wear, which he considers a nitpicking waste of time. He motions for Serena to wait.

Her gaze takes in the overstuffed chair and the rusty bicycle with a twisted front wheel. "Was this once a Goodwill shop? Did they leave stuff behind?"

"Okay, Darcy, okay, it'll all be in there, fabrics, design et cetera."
He hangs up. "Hi," he says warily, wondering what Serena's presence
could mean. He did not catch her opening salvo.

Since his move here, their conversations have bottomed out at
more-or-less civil phone calls and emails about household matters.
Never a hint from his wife about, say, where she sees their
marriage in five years.

"What did you say that upset Max so much?"

"When?" Ezra asks, mentally thumbing through twenty years
of uneasy conversations with his son.

"Ezra, I really don't have the patience for this."

"Could you be more specific?"

"Three days ago. Max moved back to L.A. He came here
intending to apologize for whatever it was he said to you in
New York."

"He never came here."

"Here, there, wherever you had the encounter. Don't play your
word games."

"Honestly, I don't know what you're talking about. I didn't
even know he was in town."

"He finally had it with New York and cooking and older
women, until his confrontation with you made him positively
furious and sent him right back there again. He phoned me from
LAX to announce that anyplace you live is toxic territory. I want
to know what happened."

What happened in Boston, Willy? Ezra has been taking pills to
keep him working and pills to make him sleep, he has been pepper-
sprayed and had a car drop on him, but surely he would have
noticed so fateful an encounter with his son.

"Serena, I have not seen or spoken to Max. Honestly. I'd
remember."

"So he's a liar? Hallucinating? What?"

"Let's settle this."

He phones Max, who answers with, "Go fuck yourself. And
never call me again."

"Wait, it's me," Ezra says, on the chance he's been taken for a telemarketer.

"I know."And hangs up.

Serena's glare informs him that she heard.

"Didn't refresh my memory," he says, with instant regret.

"That was a joke."

She does not smile. "Must've been pretty nasty. Both of you unwilling to discuss it."

"Goddamn it, I'm as confused as you are.'

"So be it, Ezra. You made your bed." She starts out, then turns. "I'm refinancing again. They'll messenger you the papers to sign."

"I have not seen Max since New York."

"Sign."

Ezra to Ariadne Koppos: Hallucination?
Max told his mother he had a traumatic encounter with me here in L.A. It never happened. Any idea what this is about?

Ariadne Koppos to Ezra: Max
He clams up when I press him on it. But I sincerely doubt you're capable—at least not intentionally—of the sort of cold-blooded callousness he hints at.

Are you still self-medicating?

In any case, he does overreact. Give him time. Whatever's going on, at least it's persuaded him to finally enroll in the CIA. He'll be moving into an apartment closer to the school, sharing costs with a couple of girls his own age. Traded me in for two twenties, you might say, and I am delighted. Though I'll miss him.

You Popkin men do have your quirky charm.

Are you having second thoughts about the kidney? You CAN change your mind. Honestly, I'd understand. I have a possible back-up donor, a second cousin on my father's side in Detroit.

Ezra to Ariadne Koppos: All's well
Of course I haven't changed my mind. What kind of man do you think I am?

Ezra to Dr. Sidney Fingerman: Dumbdumbdumb
What kind of man do I think I am?

Ariadne gave me a way out of the kidney donation. Did I sing hallelujahs to a universe that takes my side for a change?

Hah! I shot back some garbage suggesting my word is my bond.

I am disgusted with me.

As is my son, by the way. He suddenly finds me an abomination far beyond our workaday acrimony. Disturbing enough. But the cause, which he will only hint at, is so imaginary I worry about him.

This new twist in our relationship consumes me. I find myself incorporating this material into my current writing project, god help me.

Darcy is less than enchanted with wailing monologs on paternal woes and angry father-son confrontations. GET BACK ON TRACK she emails him. THIS CRAP IS A REAL DOWNER, WE'RE AFTER MASS AUDIENCE NOT KING LEAR GROUPIES. DID YOU LUNCH ON EXLAX?

But Ezra can think of nothing else. With that subject censored, writer's block sets in. No, he tells himself, I am not using Max to avoid writing, I am a father whose son loathes him with no apparent motive. This is a reasonable obsession.

He calls New York again. Max, who picks up instantly twenty-four hours a day, sends dad to voicemail. Ditto for a follow-up call. An email is equally stonewalled. Clever Ezra borrows a cell phone from good neighbor Ghupta to avoid caller ID, and at last hears his son's, "Hello?"

Ezra rattles off words at the speed of side-effects warnings on drug commercials. "I never saw you here how could you claim to your mother Max I need to—"

Click.

Next morning Ezra wakes from another tormented night to find an email from Max.

Max Popkin to Ezra: Twisted
Didn't say you saw me. Said I saw you.

Walked into your office thinking I owed you an apology. Nobody around. I hear this groaning & shrieking from your back room. Peek in and shit it was disgusting you and some woman going at it.

Always knew you were twisted but man I never figured positions like that. Sickest of all was even while screwing you were still pecking away at your laptop!

Like I needed more proof that your writing trumps every normal human emotion.

You're lucky I don't want to hurt Mom. Now stay out of my life.

If Ezra's neighbors hear his hysterical laughter they think nothing of it, not coming from this oddball tenant, who lately has been letting slip the news that he's about to donate a kidney for a friend. "It's the kind of thing you do, right?"

Ezra spends half the morning editing and polishing an email to Max explaining his misinterpretation of the scene. And, can you believe it, Max, this massage thing you saw is so effective your neurotic dad is actually writing without a partner. (Though, at a low point he almost joined forces with a writer who ultimately partnered with his thirteen-year-old son instead—as a bar mitzvah gift! This business!)

He wishes Max success in his career as a cook and will be sending a small congratulatory check. Invest in stock, he advises, veal or chicken, it's up to you.

Ezra shoots off the email and returns to Darcy's script reborn.

That evening he phones Serena to explain Max's laughable misunderstanding vis-à-vis the massage.

"He bought that?" Serena responds coolly.

"It's the truth. You don't believe me, talk to Betsiross yourself."

"Betsy Ross? Really?"

"My Thai masseuse. Yes. And it's just a massage, Serena, nothing else."

"Whatever you say."

"I say a couple of sessions a week keep me writing. Used to need her three times a day but I've tapered off."

"I'm starting to believe it has to be massage after all."

"Don't be snarky."

"Well, I hope Max is okay with your explanation."

"Me, too. In any case he seems to be straightening himself out. By the way, did Stefan tell you I thanked him for the job? I misjudged the guy."

"Actually, he was quite moved by your apology. That was decent of you."

"Darcy may be kinky when it comes to details, but she draws character depths and dramatic insights out of me I never knew I had. How's Xanadu coming along?"

"The main design element is blowing everybody away, so we've renamed it 'Stilt Haus.' Two shelter magazines and a film maker are documenting the construction."

"Congratulation. Honestly. Look, can we have dinner sometime soon? An old-fashioned date?"

"Ezra, I'd love to, but my schedule—"

"I've changed."

"Let me get back to you."

Ezra works long hours now. One day he realizes that it's been almost two weeks since Darcy called or sent her frequent good-cop-bad-cop email or summoned him for a meeting. He phones her but is not put through. His messages go unreturned. Panic building in him like Old Faithful, he bicycles to the studio.

"Your name isn't on the list today," says the guard who has so often lifted the gate for him. At his request the guard phones the WhipDarce office to clear things up. "Sorry, Mr. Popkin, they say they can't see you."

Back in his office a trembling Ezra phones his agent for clarification.

"I know, I know," Brad says without clarifying, "but look at it this way, you're a few bucks ahead, you got a recent credit. Not bad for someone in your demographic. I can say that, can't I? Demographic?"

"I'm off the project?"

"Shit. Didn't she tell you? You were replaced by the writer Darcy had writing behind you."

"When?"

"Two weeks ago. Ezra, forgive me, I assumed—"

"But she loved my work."

"Don't they all. But I have to tell you, buddy, coming into meetings schlepping a rusty old bicycle doesn't exactly inspire confidence."

"Somebody drove my car off when I was under it. I was traumatized. I told Darcy what happened!"

"And she loved it. They're using the incident in this new crime psychologist procedural she's developing."

"Darcy stole my trauma?"

"First come, first served, you know the drill."

"I don't even know what that means."

"It means use your momentum to give me a few screenplays and we'll see what we can do. And by the way, Darcy says you once cried for an entire meeting. Goddamn it, writers are supposed to hold that back until afterwards."

"I was pepper-sprayed!"

"Darcy pepper-sprayed you?"

"My landlord did! He thought I was a burglar!"

"Like it. Develop that before somebody else does."

Ezra composes an angry email to Darcy. She responds immediately.

Darcy Whippet to Ezra: Creative differences
I feel we have become good friends during our intimate collaboration. So I know you will accept this decision that's been forced on me, and not consider our problem anything more than a minor blind spot in your otherwise brilliant talent.

The fact is, you just don't seem to understand either the characters or the thrust of your story. Draft after draft I have struggled to help you see the meaning of this complex work. Yet it never shows up on the page.

You must be equally frustrated. So I suspect you'll be relieved to learn we're bringing in a new writer, freeing you to go on to more simpatico projects.

All of us at WhipDarce Productions look forward to working with you on material better suited to your enormous talent.

Ezra to Darcy: Utter confusion
My talent is not appropriate for the play I wrote? I don't understand characters I created? None of this is in your notes. Increasingly they focus on costumes, sets and props. Did you intend some deep subtext that escaped me?

Darcy Whippet to Ezra: My bad
You have every right to be angry. I kept certain facts from you, because I wanted nothing to interfere with the depth and range of your creative reach.

This project will be the first in a series of moving dramas that will double as a living virtual mail-order catalog.

The stage manager-Greek chorus (beautifully written, Ezra) will comment not only on the characters' motives and passions, but also on their jewelry, clothing, makeup, hair styling and furnishings. A crawl will give prices and an 800 number. Some of the actual locations will also be for sale or time-share.

An interactive feature will allow viewers to re-accessorize characters and change the color and style of furnishings.

Don't blame yourself because you couldn't bring it off. This is drama for the digital age, so generational differences handicap even the most talented. One might even say that if the edge is cutting enough, experience itself is a handicap. Your replacement is an exciting young writer I discovered at his bar mitzvah. His speech told me all I needed to know! (Aren't the kids the only ones who truly understand all this?) Fortunately for me he had just broken up with his writing partner, an elderly relative of some sort.

Don't be too hard on yourself. Gutenberg would be totally flummoxed by a computer but that takes nothing from his brilliant invention of moveable type.

Ezra to Darcy Whippet: Digitize this
The Chinese had moveable type first, and I hear one or two of them are pretty good with computers. Suggest you outsource your project to a nine-year-old in Beijing.

Digitally speaking, it's been real nice knowing you. Middle digit. Extended.

Ezra to Lifshultz Heating & Air Conditioning: Lost it again
Send Drywall Man to repair latest damage to your wall.

Ditto your Fluorescent Lights Man, and your Toilet Man to open a clog
from a flushed script (Act One moved along fine, but as usual the
second act got bogged down.)

I can also use a Tinnitus Person If you have one. Emails from a
deranged producer have set my ears ringing non-stop. Relief comes
only from hitting my head against the wall (see first paragraph).

Ezra sits at his computer determined to follow Brad's advice—
use that momentum to churn out scripts.

Days of false starts and dead ends follow, of blank screens and
aimless bicycle rides through heavy traffic.

Now he lies listless under Betsiross's ministrations. The masseuse
is worried by his silence.

"Hmmm?" she says pointedly.

"This is the last time. I can't afford you anymore."

"Okay. Give you a freebie sometime when work is slow."

"Your English is getting better."

"I listen hard to you. Watch lots TV. Must be exciting to write
all that crazy shit."

"It's a living," he lies. And waits for the inevitable next question.

"Where you get your ideas?" Bingo.

"I don't. You see, Betsiross, I am the definition of 'crazy.' I
keep repeating the same thing but expect a different result."

"Hmmm."

"You can say that again." He sits up. "Well, I have to get
back to it."

And so another week passes of fits and starts, starts and fits
and a back window shattered by a flying stapler. Then one morning, after avoiding work via the *L.A. Times*, the online *N.Y. Times*
and its online crossword puzzle, Ezra encounters an outrage in
Daily Variety that leaves him gasping for breath.

He shouts this outrage into Brad's voicemail and demands an
immediate investigation. Fearing he may have been less than
coherent, he sends a follow-up email.

Ezra to Brad, Talent Central: Thieves!
Trades today report screenplay about Lincoln coming back from the dead for revenge fetching $900k. Damn thing is called HONESTLY, ABE.

Sounds exactly the same as the FOUR SCORE AND LIFE screenplay we pitched to P. Bretton Woods. This cannot be a coincidence! Did any spouse, manager, lover, pimp, etc. connected to the principals of this HONESTLY ABE project lay eyes on ours? They must have!

Brad, Talent Central, to Ezra: Paranoia
Bad news on the Lincoln script. Really looks like coincidence instead of the usual larceny. The agent is some East Coast shlepper who lucked out. Ditto the writer, a first-timer named Gavin Pulsky. Kid used to be a furniture mover.

Ezra to Brad, Talent Central: Sue the fucker
THAT SON OF A BITCH WAS THE MOVER AT P. BRETTON WOODS' HOUSE. BACK AND FORTH FOR MOST OF MY PITCH. FIND ME A KILLER PLAGIARISM LAWYER TO NAIL THE THIEVING BASTARD'S HIDE TO THE WALL.

Brad, Talent Central, to Ezra: Suicidal
Forget lawyers. You'd drown in legal fees and never win anyway. Plus nobody hires troublemakers. Especially not with your recent Stanley/Darcy craziness.

Think positive—this sale proves your ideas are still marketable. You go, girl!

Ezra seethes. He wraps his new blood pressure cuff around his arm, a recent addition to his work-avoidance tool kit. What are those numbers? Has to be defective.

He takes deep calming breaths. Makes an urgent call to Betsiross. Unavailable! Fuck, nine hundred thousand! But I will not plummet into self-pity. The universe is a miracle, it spawns stars, galaxies, shits, liars, frauds and thieves in the night. I remain what I am, a good writer slightly blocked, never defeated.

(Idea for short story? Man kidnaps plagiarist, ties hands behind his back, forces him to copy Shakespeare's entire canon with crayon strapped to his penis.)

Any chance Brad might be right, this plagiarism at least proves they are viable writers? A lousy price to pay for that insight, nine hundred big ones, that robbing bastard shit Gavin, may he rot in hell.

Yet if Stanley buys this it would destroy his reason for giving up, ease him back into the fold. Ezra spends the afternoon in a writing frenzy, crafting an email to Stanley that combines outrage with seduction worthy of Casanova.

Before he can send it an email arrives that blows his plan out of the water, along with his view of reality.

BunnKumfi di Milano to Ezra Popkin: Chair problem
Dear Mr. Popkin,

The chair that so pained you appears to be our Benvenuto Cellini model, of solid African bubinga wood (US $1137.00).

As makers of quality furnishings since 1723, pride of craftsmanship lives in the hearts of all our 329 workers so I am dismayed that you and a "tuchus" suffered such distress (did you intend this word? I fail to find it in my Dictionary).

It is a sad truth of our tragic human existence that not all persons integrate with all objects.

But I assure you, at bottom our chair is a true masterwork of utilitarian art by an exciting new design genius, Stanley Blitz. We intend an entire line by him. I, as Director of Design, and even prior as a fashion model, have never met an artistic sensibility who so brilliantly harmonizes "the common touch" with stylistic boldness.

I have passed numerous intimate moments with this charming person during visits to your country. Can you believe that so talented an artisan was formerly a cinema writer? Truly, there are Renaissance Men still!

Most sincerely,
Sophia Donato, Director of Design

Dizzy Ezra reads the email a second time and then a third. It cannot be saying what it appears to say. He parses the message with the care of a Talmudic scholar, searching for evidence that it masks a scheme by Nigerian swindlers to relieve him of his life savings.

Yet no "good faith deposit of $10,000" is requested, no deposed ruler begs his help in smuggling gold ingots out of his country.

There can be only one meaning, however surreal. Stanley's chairs are selling at $1137 a pop. Further, he spends "intimate moments"—my god, what can that mean?—with some sexy long-legged Italian beauty.

After many fumbles with the phone keypad Ezra reaches his wife.

"Just learned Stanley's responsible for that conference room chair of yours," he groans. "Why didn't you tell me?"

"I doubted you'd take it well, my helping his career along. Sounds like I was right."

"You think me that petty?"

"Since you ask."

"Not my business where you buy chairs. Though I could say a word about your taste."

"You might as well know all. I did more for Stanley than just that chair."

"Good god, you sprang for a table, too?"

"I arranged for him to meet BunnKumfi's head of design when she came to a furniture show in North Carolina. The company knows me. I've recommended clients for years."

"You and Stefan are a real pair of humanitarians, always out there lending a helping hand."

"Stefan had the best intentions for you with Darcy! Don't blame him because you screwed up."

"You sure do step up fast to defend him against me. Are you that tight with all your clients?"

"You cried during meetings with Darcy's team. Then finished off the relationship with a 'fuck you' email."

"Wow. From Darcy to Stefan to you, faster than a speeding cabal. Are you aware that Darcy had a hidden agenda? I was unwittingly adapting my play into a clothing catalog."

"What?"

"Oh, well, why not, in a universe where Stanley can strike gold with a chair only Torquemada could love?"

"Do you take no pleasure at all in what Stanley's accomplished?

Are you that bitter?"

"Hey, who can argue with success?" His voice becomes a growling mutter. "Unless it's by some goddamn furniture-moving thief."

"Stanley's work *is* good, Ezra."

"Oh, way better than good. Renaissance quality, he's a man for all seasons. And to think he used drive me crazy playing with our office thermostat."

"Well, I suppose you'll just have to be upset. Now I do have to go."

"My lunch invitation is still open."

"Both our lives are in flux right now. Let's see how things shake out."

"What things?"

"I mean I'm not ready to make any decisions."

"Lunch is not a decision. It's a sandwich."

"Gotta go. Things are really crazy here."

She hangs up. He holds the phone absently and stares up at the cracked ceiling. Ezra Popkin. Always the last to know. It is not enough to fail, one's friends must succeed. No, that can't be it. Hell, close enough. And why did she defend Stefan so passionately? What the fuck is going on between them?

He feels an urgent need to contact Dr. Fingerman. Except was he also in the know? Ezra imagines Doc F. helping out in the wood shop while Stanley-stiltskin spins his dross into gold.

"Sid," says Stanley, "as a mental health professional, you think my overnight international success will make Ezra miserable?"

Fingerman looks up from his broom. "Better way to do it, Stan. Remember that napkin ring you wove out of splinters I tweezed from your fingers? A matched set could fetch at least a thousand on Rodeo Drive."

"Great idea, Sid, I'll have Sophia run off a bunch, and full-page it in The New Yorker. *Absolutely guarantee Ezra's life is crap."*

The hammer of fists on Ezra's back door interrupts his musing. He opens the triple locks and a hysterical Betsiross bursts in with two other masseuses.

"Immigration!" she says in an urgent whisper.

Ezra hustles the trio into his airplane-sized bathroom and rushes up front to peek out his window blinds. Next door ICE officers lead other masseuses into a black van. He waits several minutes after it drives off then hurries into Forever Joyous Thai Massage. Only the owner is there, on the phone speaking crisply in a foreign tongue. The conversation goes back and forth and finally she nods, says something conclusive and hangs up.

"New staff here tomorrow," she says.

"Immigration come here often?"

"Only when my son-a-bitch competition tip them off."

"Betsiross and two others are in my bathroom."

"No kidding? Mr. Popkin, you win a bunch of massages. How that movie of yours going?"

"I'll tell them the coast is clear."

Ezra's announcement is greeted with hugs and tears and, from one of he masseuses, a seductively whispered offer in a language he is relieved not to comprehend.

Next day at noon she delivers her lagniappe. He savors it alone in the back room, a thermos full of home-made tom ka gai soup. In mid-slurp he hears the tinkling of bells from someone opening his front door.

"Hello?" an unseen man inquires. "Ezra Popkin? You here?"

(Immigration come back? *Sir, we have reason to believe that you habitually hide illegal aliens in your bathroom. This means life, Popkin!*) The curtains between front and back part. In steps a man of perhaps fifty wearing worn jeans and a sweatshirt, with expensive hair and a jaw that could stand in for the Rock of Gibraltar.

"Stefan Jibbet, man. Found myself in the neighborhood. My Ferrari guy's down the street."

Thrown by the man's chutzpah, Ezra can only manage the punch line of an old joke.

"So what're you selling this time, cancer?"

"I swear, Darcy didn't intend to go that route with your play. But it 'jes grew,' you know, like Topsy."

"Topsy who?"

"Uncle Tom's Cabin?"

"Darcy also adapting that? Eliza jumping ice floes wearing the latest winter fashions?"

Ezra returns to his soup.

"Ezra, I live with envy all the time and I accept it. What I can't stand is someone hating me for the wrong reason. I really figured I was helping you."

"You used the word 'I' five times in as many seconds. Really ought to discuss that with your therapist."

"Just hear me out. It concerns my latest directing gig. A true story about this Russian immigrant who once spied for the CIA in the Soviet Union. After seventeen years in a Siberian Gulag freezing his toes off he escapes by dog sled just in time to help Gorbachev create glasnost. I tell you, this guy Yuri is *Dr. Zhivago* meets *Gone with the Wind*."

"Yuri?" Ezra dreads the answer. "Yuri who?"

"I forget, something Russian I think. Service manager at a car dealer before Disney paid zillions for his life story. Crazy son of a bitch worries I don't change my oil often enough."

Ezra's jaw drops. His eyes widen. A single tear rolls down each cheek.

"Go away," he growls through quivering lips.

"Here's my point. Next week I go to Russia to scout locations."

"Out. Now."

"Serena's taking a vacation from architecture to come along as my right-hand man on the film. Everything will be totally professional. That's what I need you to understand."

"My wife is going to Russia. With you?"

"I've never done a film of this scope. I need her eyes, her unique visual imagination."

"So it's Serena's eyes you're after," Ezra notes blankly.

"Knowing you're okay with this would mean a lot to me, Ezra. Because Serena's really excited about this new direction."

"'Nude erection'? Why did you say 'nude erection'?"

"I said 'new direction,' Ezra, a fresh challenge for her talent."

"I heard you say 'nude erection,' you slimy bastard."

"Man, I'm only trying to do the friendly thing here. I admire

Serena purely as a talented…"

Ezra is emitting an almost subsonic growl.

Stefan backs away. "What's happening to your face? Shit! You probably did try to garrote your best friend."

"Are you fucking my wife?" Ezra shrieks.

"No!"

"I think you're fucking my wife!"

Stefan sprints for his car. He shouts back at Ezra, "If I was, guess who'd be the last to know, you ungrateful schmuck!"

Multiple emotions whiplash Ezra, dominated by a sour sense of déjà vu. A full day passes before he's under control enough to confront Serena.

His call gets through immediately. Guilt? "Hi," she says. "I've been meaning to call you."

"About what?"

"To apologize for Stefan's bull-in-the-china-shop act. It was well intentioned, it really was. Though I should've been the one to tell you my plans."

"About your plans. Still a bit confused on that."

"The timing is right for me to try this. My other projects are winding down and construction is on hold at Stilt Haus while we wait for a volcanic eruption in Indonesia to cool down. Stefan insists that particular lava rock is the only material for his atrium walls. So I'm dipping my toe into show biz. How about that. Your wife the Associate Producer."

"So off to Russia you go then, you and the china shop bull. Associating and producing."

"Take it as you like, Ezra. I will no longer have this sort of discussion with you."

"Am I not entitled to an opinion?"

"If you were rational, yes. Don't worry, when I'm back in a few weeks we'll have a really nice long talk."

Her threat hangs in the air distorting Ezra's thought processes long after the phone call. In the days that follow Serena's departure he grows increasingly detached from reality.

The bizarre action to which this leads him, the state of mind that made it seem perfectly rational, are best explained by the following statement prepared for Dr. Fingerman.

Letter via U.S. Postal Service to Dr. Sidney Fingerman, for purposes that may soon become evident:

With no one expecting me anywhere at any time in the foreseeable future (save that kidney-shaped time bomb), I had unlimited hours to stoke my bitterness and anger. At a wandering (in several senses) wife. At believing I could swim with sharks and survive. At scorning Yuri Potemkin's offer of fifty-percent of his life. At Sophia Donato for making Stanley's dream come true. Even at you, Dr. Fingerman, for fraternizing with the enemy. Matters came to a head one night when Betsiross approached me in the middle of our mini-mall's parking lot. Apparently I was standing there gesturing and speaking to no visible person.

"Ezra, maybe you come inside now? Nice massage?"

Startled out of my reverie, I quickly invented the latest smart phone, which I explained was miniaturized to the point of invisibility and hurried into my office shaken to the core.

Enough, I told myself. You are losing it. You must look ahead not backwards. Keep the mind challenged and diverted to stave off early dementia.

I have always harbored a secret passion to play the harpsichord. If not now, when? The question was settled in the negative the next day in the middle of my first lesson, with an offer of double my money back if I left immediately and never returned.

Despair settled in again until the night I awoke from restless sleep recalling that I was the owner of a chainsaw. I found it awaiting me seductively in a corner among unpacked possessions.

Here was my road to mental health and even new career horizons. Not so elevated as the harpsichord, but there had to be a fair amount of skill involved. I would master the chainsaw, then move on to more challenging devices with ever greater electronic aspects, until I was able to sidle into the digital age before anyone noticed.

The instruction manual was useless, all dry, academic prose. "The only way you're going to understand this thing," I told myself (we were on speaking terms again), "is through hands-on experience."

But what to practice on? Where could I slice, cut and chop without damaging anything of consequence? Even as the question formed, the answer came to me. Which is why late that evening I stood in the moonlight looking up at the curved stilts supporting Stefan Jibbet's hilltop house.

I jerked out the saw's starter rope and it roared to life, an eager, angry creature. An orgiastic thrill went through me as I applied the voraciously racing chain to a stilt.

The next thing I knew I was tumbling down the hill, flailing for a hand-hold.

I had overlooked one critical detail: those damned stilts were made of steel. Trying to sever one had produced an ear-piercing screech and a cascade of sparks that scared the

bejeezers out of me, while the saw and I flew
off in different directions.

   Bloodied I may have been, but my chainsaw was
itching for more. A madman now, I pedaled
through the night to my own house on stilts,
whose mistress was far away doing the Russian
two-steppe.

   I double-checked: these stilts were
definitely solid wood. My saw sliced through
them lickety-split, first one stilt, then a
second. I leapt aside barely in time to avoid
death by falling bathtub, as with a snap,
crackle and pop our house collapsed into its
final remodel.

   There you have it, Doctor Fingerman. Use this
information as you see fit.

Later, snugly back on his inflatable mattress, Ezra contemplates
with a smile Serena's reaction when she learns of their house's
demise. A touch of remorse creeps in, but briefly, and he has his
first good night's sleep in weeks. It is only the next morning that
he realizes the true horror of his deed when awakened by a phone
call from Luanne.

   "Have you seen Stanley?" she asks without preamble.

   "No. Should I?"

   "He's been in L.A. the past three days for one of his bloody
furniture conventions. But he stopped answering my calls."

   "Okay, what hotel's he at?"

   "Didn't Serena tell you before she left? He's at your place."

   "My house?"

   "Oh, what the fuck, Ezra, you might as well know, things have
been awful between us. We barely talk. He's off in his own world,
and it keeps moving further away from mine. Sometimes I think
Stanley's having an affair. Is that crazy?"

   "Stanley was in my house last night?"

"I shouldn't have bothered you. Forget it."

"I'll swing by."

"Don't tell him I was worried, okay?"

"Mum's the word." Ezra races to the collapsed house. Yellow tape surrounds the rubble. A police car and a fire truck stand by. Ezra demands a search of the rubble. The officer in charge, Detective Sanchez, assures him this has already been done and no bodies have been found alive or otherwise.

Ezra begs them in a in a mildly hysterical way to look again, and rushes past to move debris himself. Strong, insistent hands lead him back to a police car.

Detective Sanchez points out the sawn-off stilts (Ezra displays proper horror) and asks why the Popkins were not at home last night. Ezra briefs the detective on their marital and career situations.

"Any idea who might have done this to your house?"

"I have no enemies," replies Simple Simon.

"What about Mrs. Popkin?"

"We have our differences. But I wouldn't say 'enemy'."

"Where can we reach her?"

"Russia. She's working on a movie about the life of my car mechanic. Kind of a funny story there."

"I'm sure. Anyway, we have a suspect in custody. Rather not say who it is right now. We'll be in touch."

Huh? Is this a ruse to throw Ezra off guard? And if Stanley wasn't here last night, where was he? Snug as a bug in Sophia Donato's hotel room?

The answer comes that afternoon when Stanley bursts into Ezra's storefront.

"You crazy bastard! Do you resent my success so much you'd destroy your own house to get at me?"

"Wasn't me, Stanley. They have a suspect locked up."

"That suspect was me." Stanley collapses onto a chair. "Jeezus, this has been the worst twelve hours of my life."

"You want a massage?"

"Have you gone completely over the edge?"

"Were you in the house or not?"

"Yes! Until your fucking chainsaw woke me up!"

Stanley tells of being shocked awake in the middle of the night by a chainsaw that seemed to be right there with him in the dark bedroom.

He stumbles to the window and looks down to see Ezra in the moonlight sawing away at a stilt. Stanley's shouts are drowned out by the saw. A naked sleeper, he rushes outside without clothing himself, by which time Ezra has moved on to a new stilt.

Suddenly the house starts to collapse in front of Stanley, in horrible, mesmerizing slow motion.

He spots Ezra running off to a bike in the shadows and pedaling away. He, himself, can only stand there naked and shaking, scared shitless, struggling to process what he has just witnessed.

The eerie quiet is broken by the sound of approaching sirens. A pair of police cars screech to a stop, pinning him in the crossfire of their headlights. There is an amplified command.

"Drop your weapon!"

"What weapon?"

"Drop it, sir! Right now!"

Stanley realizes he has picked up the abandoned chainsaw. He drops it. They hustle him handcuffed into the back seat of a police car, toss a blanket over his nudity and deposit him in a holding cell for the night.

"You ever been in a holding cell, Ezra, with a guy named 'Buzzard' who has a swastika tattoos on his nose, and wants to be your best friend?"

"Try to understand, this thing that happened was not about you."

"It did not 'happen!' You did it. I saw you!"

"But you didn't tell the police that, right?" More prayer than query.

"What the hell do you think I told them? See you 'round, buddy. And if you run across Buzzard, mention my name. He'll treat you right."

And with that sally Stanley is gone, leaving behind only his sly smile.

Ezra to Dr.Sidney Fingerman: Department of Defense

I have mailed you a statement detailing my state of mind prior to the destruction of our stilted home last night. If I stand trial because of this 3AM shenanigan—and doubtless will, now that Stanley's immersion in things Italian has given him a taste for VENDETTA—I would like you to back up my plea of temporary sanity.

Yes. Sanity. In a world gone mad, where the improbable had become the soup du jour, reason compelled me to jolt the system back on track. Just as a pair of high-voltage paddles applied to someone's chest might seem anti-social, yet can be the best medicine.

So I free you of your vow of confidentiality (I'll even toss in two other vows of your choice—chastity, obedience, etc. Have some fun for a change). Reveal all when the moment arrives. I am not a monster.

Detective Sanchez shows up the next morning as Ezra returns to his storefront with his AM coffee and bagel.

"We were able to track down Mrs. Popkin in Russia, through her office. I'm surprised you didn't already inform her about your house."

"We live separately."

"Right. You did say that. Nice setup you got here, by the way."

"How'd she take it?"

"Not well. Said she couldn't talk anymore and needed to lay down after hearing the awful news. She handed me off to—" Sanchez consults notes, "—a Mr. Stefan Jibbet."

"Lay down? Were they in a hotel room?"

"Can't say, it was a cell phone. You think something's going on between your wife and Mr. Jibbet?"

"Not my business anymore."

"Anyway, she assured me through him, from the bed or wherever she was, that she had no idea who might have reason to destroy your place. Same as you. You people must be a couple of saints."

Why doesn't he get to the point? Is there something in the Detective Manual that says you have to play this cat-and-mouse game—a scene Ezra has written once or twice himself—before slapping on the cuffs? I did it, you know it, I know it, cut the crap! Still, Ezra resists the urge to confess. That would be cheating.

"Incidentally, Mr. Popkin, we had to release our original suspect because of new information."

"Stanley told me. He used to be my writing partner. What new information?"

"Little acrimony between you two, right? Maybe even physical confrontations?"

"Not really. Stanley's always been high-strung, imaginative. Lives in his emotions. That's what made him such a great writer."

Hold it. How credible is an accusation from a man found naked, holding the guilty chainsaw? There's a word for that. Crazy. And crazy people say crazy things.

"Fortunately, Mr. Blitz's story was corroborated by another witness."

Oops. "Who?"

"Your neighbor, a Mrs. Bluntly."

"Ah, yes, Mrs. Bluntly." Eyes so keen she can spot one leaf from a Popkin tree landing on her property, with accusatory notes to follow.

"She called 911. Your house collapsing woke her up. She saw someone running away into the shadows, and Mr. Blitz standing there naked. Same story he told us."

"And this person running away—?" Okay, time to polish me off.

"Neither witness gave us anything useful. Too dark."

"Really?"

"Piece of luck, huh? I mean for the malicious scum who did this."

"They get all the breaks."

"So it would seem. But don't you worry, we aren't giving up on this. You will definitely hear from me again."

They shake hands.

"Thanks, Detective. Appreciate your coming by."

Detective Sanchez cocks his head sideways and aims a finger at Ezra.

"You hear yourself, sir? You said *your* coming by. Most of us would say *you* coming by, right? That's why I like talking to writers. I always learn something."

"Are you doing Columbo?"

"We all have our heroes." He starts out, then turns. "By the way, Mr. Popkin, you wouldn't mind coming down to the station to be fingerprinted, would you?"

He winks.

"Seriously?"

"Very seriously, sir."

Ezra promises, knowing he never touched the chainsaw without gloves.

Once alone he emails Stanley to compliment him on a game well played. Torturing Ezra with false threats, indeed! (Crafting his message with care to avoid self-incrimination in the eyes of unintended readers.)

That evening Ezra receives an agitated phone call from Luanne.

"Ezra you rotten bastard, Stanley left me, and all thanks to you. How could you do this to me again? How could you?" She starts crying.

"What do you mean?"

"Oh, come on. Chopping down your house? He told me the whole story. You've done some crazy shit over the years, but this is so hurtful even for you, so irresponsible."

"But how did that—"

"He's grateful to you for what happened that night. I don't know if he's crazy or you're crazy. All I know is he's running off to Italy to live with his furniture bimbo."

Ezra to Stanley Blitz: Have you lost your mind?
Why did you walk out on Luanne? And why the fuck does she think I'm responsible? What is going on?

Stanley to Ezra: Thank you
I've left Luanne and, yes, in your own idiot way you made it possible.

I met a woman last year at a home furnishings convention. There was a powerful attraction between us, but we stifled our emotions, determined to remain furniture professionals when our paths crossed afterwards.

This week at the L.A. show our feelings were overwhelming. Yet neither of us had the courage to take the next step. I slept in your house to avoid the temptation of being in a hotel room anywhere near hers.

Then your house collapsed and I escaped death by seconds (no thanks to you). I came out of that with a powerful sense of the capriciousness of life, how vital it is to make every day count.

I survived that miserable night in jail by concentrating on Sophia. Life with my beautiful Sophia.

We had a long talk after they let me go and she agreed it was stupid and cruel to waste any more time. I have since moved into her hotel room. When this show closes we return to Italy together.

Mille grazie!

Ezra to Stanley: Listen to yourself

You're shaken, as well you should be. But once again you've made a life-altering decision in haste. Be man enough to discuss this with Luanne. Because my impression is that in the giddiness of success you have forgotten what's important.

Stanley, you are ill-cast as a lovesick puppy. (Puppy's best friend, ok.) Consider—just consider—that you might be a victim of middle-age panic and the allure of distant cultures. Take a breath, think this through.

At least give me ten minutes. Restaurant of your choice—but this time on your dime. After all, who's famous on seven continents? Can we just do that little thing?

Stanley to Ezra: Do not screw with this

What qualifies you to be my life coach?

Assaulting me twice in our office and my workshop, hare-brained schemes with a Wall St. nut case, an affair with my wife (which may or may not be only in the past, given your demonstrated lack of humanity)?

I hate what I'm doing to Luanne. But if you ever met Sophia (don't count on it) you'd understand. She has a tragic sense of life, realizes that today is everything, risk is all there is.

If I haven't mentioned it before, my warmest thanks.

It is late the next day before Luanne answers Ezra's many phone calls.

"Hey, Ezra. How's it going?" She sounds improbably chipper.

"I've been trying to reach you since yesterday. Are you okay?"

"I just bought the most gorgeous aubergine Mercedes convertible."

"Why?"

"They have prettier colors than BMW. And I found someone to buy all that woodworking crap of his. You wouldn't believe how much it was worth."

"Have you been drinking?"

"Ezra, this is working out so perfectly. To quote my late husband, thank you, thank you, thank you."

My god, they're both certifiable. "Great, enjoy. But this adventure of Stanley's will not last, understand that."

"Don't give a flying fuck. Speaking of which, remember how we used to wonder about doing it in an airplane? If you're still interested I can drive to L.A. in my lovely new aubergine Mercedes convertible and—"

"With the husband of your best friend? Really?"

"Not really."

"Thank you."

"I meant the husband part. Oops."

"Oops?"

"Serena and I talked for the longest time. Oh, Ezra, you and me, we are suddenly so birds of a feather. What time is it there?"

"We're in the same time zone. What did Serena tell you?"

"Gotta go, they're waiting for me at happy hour. Bye, Ezra. Cheep cheep."

Details of Luanne's hint arrive almost immediately, via an email from Serena.

Serena Popkin to Ezra: The End
You polished off more than our home. This marriage is over.

I won't even begin to ask why you did it. I don't care why you did it.

And don't bother denying it because even though I'm half a world away from the scene of your crime, I am 100% certain it was you.

Luanne tells me Stanley's left her. Apparently you had a hand in that, too. You do leave a trail of wreckage in your wake.

Complicate our divorce and I will turn you in.

Ezra to Serena: Crime & Punishment
Too late. I got to the cops first.

As I explained to Detective Sanchez, after so many remodels and additions you had no place left to go but down, all the way down to a level playing field.

The insurance company's pockets being deeper than your own, you engaged the services of a professional home-wrecker whose day job is knee-capping actors & writers. He hired an underling to do the dirty work then fled the country with you.

Detective Sanchez agrees with me that you have acted with a chilling lack of love, fidelity and human decency.

Incidentally, who introduced Stanley to this woman for whom he's abandoned Launne? Ah, yes. Nice work.

As for an uncomplicated divorce, fine with me. You can have the house.

Ezra feels deep satisfaction with the dispatch of this email, but his mood erupts into fury when his in-box reveals a new message lying in wait:

Billing Dept. Sunimitsu Heavy Industries to Ezra Popkin:
FINAL NOTICE
Re: Silver Gables Retirement Residence, Occupant #86520-Q

Arrears Payment in form of Certified Check must be received by midnight of above date or Eviction Proceedings will be initiated.

"My heart burns like fire,
but my soul offers no antacid."
Masaru Kuriama,
Founder & President, Sunimitsu Industries.

Ezra to Billing Department, Sunimitsu Heavy Industries:
Anyone home?

I made that payment, which you morons applied to a mythical car lease. Nonetheless I am FedExing a new check from my dwindling assets to guarantee that you do not have your way with my mother.

That check is #937.

Say it.

"Check #937 is for Occupant #86520-Q."

I can't hear you.

"CHECK #937 IS FOR OCCUPANT #86520-Q."

"Louder!

"CHECK #937 IS FOR OCCUPANT #86520-Q, SIR!"

Email confirmation within twenty-four hours or I will sue your ass off.

Composing this broadside inspires Ezra to further literary effort.

Ezra to Sophia Donato, BunKumfi di Milano:
Our mutual friend

I was shocked when your email told me that the Stanley Blitz I have known for many years as a friend and writing partner is now a famous chair designer.

But that's just like Stanley. A man of many secrets. Imagine, we worked together forever before I learned he had fathered seven children by his first two wives and a few other women.

His ability to deceive while seeming the most honest, gentle person in the world served us well in Hollywood. I can't count how many stories we sold that I later learned he had stolen from other writers. This is common in our business, so I doubt you have to worry that Stanley's chair design was anything but his own, most likely.

A word of caution. Don't leave him alone with expensive art books. Stanley will furtively slice out pages he wants for inspiration, with the straight razor he always carries (he cherishes sharp instruments—his nickname for this razor is "Eric the Red"). Unfortunately if you try to discuss any of his peccadilloes, whether it's this petty theft or his sexually transmitted diseases, he will claim someone has a personal vendetta against him.

He truly believes this, just as he believes that his wealthy first wife did not die under suspicious circumstances. But when police recently reopened the case he became extremely agitated.

"I won't answer any more of their questions," he told me, nervously rolling a pair of ball bearings in one hand. "Why won't they leave me alone? I should get out of the country, go somewhere they can't reach me. Maybe Italy. Yes. That's where I'll go. I've always liked Italians, they don't ask questions."

Sorry for going on like this. I remember Stanley with only warmth and gratitude. He did me no harm, never, not intentionally.

Ezra notices with alarm an aubergine Mercedes convertible coming to a stop outside his storefront office. He prays Luanne is not here to initiate him into the Mile High Club.

It's a long minute before her car door opens and she enters.

"I can't do it," she says, near tears.

"Oh good. Do what?"

"I thought I had the courage, but…" She takes in the space with disbelief. "You actually live here? I mean, all the time?"

She pushes through the curtains to the back room. "This is it?" she calls back to him. "Eeeuw!" A cry of revulsion.

Ezra hurries back to find her peering into the bathroom.

"That is disgusting. Don't you ever clean?"

"Clean enough for the three illegal immigrants I locked up there."

"Bad taste, Ezra."

She enters the bathroom and closes the door. After a minute Ezra hears the toilet flush. She emerges, flapping her hands to air-dry them, like some flightless bird. An attractive, dangerous bird, Ezra thinks.

"There was a towel," he says.

"Not really. Oh, Ezra, I came to L.A. to confront him. Both of them. It seemed so easy in Morro Bay. Look at me. Trying to out-sexy his gorgeous Italian."

Her clothes are younger than the former Luanne's, her cleavage prominent and her hair straight out of a shampoo ad. Ezra wonders whether he might consider experimenting after all, if only an airplane lav were handy instead of his unhygienic crapper.

"Let's get out of here," he says, eager to escape. "You hungry?"

"No, but I'd kill for a good cappuccino."

The irony of her craving inspires thoughts of homicide in Ezra as well. He considers taking her to the very coffee shop she once pooh-poohed as an investment for him and Stanley, where today the line is out the door day and night.

Instead they find themselves relaxing with coffees and pastry at an outside table in the side patio of Aroma Café.

"Look at the pair of us," Luanne says. "You're basically living back in our sixth-floor walkup, and I'm, well, I'm not sure where I am, but it ain't a pretty picture."

"Age hath not withered, nor custom staled et cetera."

"Thank you."

"I meant the pastry. But you, too."

"We actually used to repartee like that, didn't we? How'd it happen, Ezra? Bing, bang, boom, and suddenly it's half over and everything's falling apart."

Ezra has an urge to commandeer one of the surrounding laptops for an emergency email: *Dr. Fingerman, how do I get out of this conversation which is making me both suicidal and horny?*

Mercifully Luanne shifts the subject. "Today's the last day of the furniture convention. If I don't confront him I'll never see Stanley again."

"Then what've you got to lose?"

"You think so?"

"Nothing ventured." He raises his cup in a farewell salute. "Go for it."

"Right, then. Off to the Convention Center we go."

"We?" *She'd better mean the royal "we."*

"Come on, Ezra. I can't manage this alone. I did save your life once."

"And how'd that work out for me? No, thanks, this is between you and Stanley."

"How dare you suddenly stop interfering in our marriage? No way. You're along for the whole ride. Walk five paces behind if you will, but you're coming with me."

Yet again Ezra is astonished at the steel hidden within the women in his life. A sudden warm shudder goes through him, either passion or terror.

He's still puzzling this out as the aubergine Mercedes speeds them downtown.

Luanne and Ezra wander the vastness of the convention hall. Some displays are already closing down but a fair number of visitors mill about.

Turning a corner they find themselves before a simulated living room with the most bizarre furniture Ezra has ever seen. A banner flanked by two Italian flags proclaims "BunnKumfi di Milano."

Stanley, sitting on what is possibly a sofa, looks up from the sandwich he's munching.

"You're wasting your time," he says.

"We never discussed it," Launne says. "You just announced this is how it has to be."

"Because I'm a different person than the one you married. It didn't work anymore. What's he doing here?"

Ezra begins, "Since you consider me somewhat responsible—"

Stanley says to Luanne, "Are you sleeping with him? You know he's not right in the head."

"We are not sleeping together! The only man I ever wanted to sleep with is you!"

A woman approaches carrying a couple of empty boxes. Her black hair is fashionably streaked with grey and she's a bit overweight.

"Stanley? Who are these people?" says Italian-accented Sophia Donato.

"I'm his wife," declares Luanne. "Who are you?"

"Which wife?" Sophia glances with amusement at Stanley, then back at Luanne. "A joke we have. I'm sorry, Mrs. Blitz. You seem a nice person, just like Stanley always says. But his mind is made up for a new life. You should, too."

"Please keep out of this."

"Sure."

Sophia starts filling a box with brochures.

"Stanley, we need to talk more than we have."

"There's nothing else to say."

"I deserve ten minutes of your time. Is that asking too much?"

"Okay. We'll talk." To Sophia he says, "Be right back."

"Meet you at the entrance we came in," Ezra says, unwilling to linger in Sophia's vicinity. "Need to check out stuff for my place, something cutting edge to add drama."

"She won't be long, Ezra," Stanley says.

"You are the Ezra Popkin?" Sophia says, her tone with its own cutting edge.

"Hi."

"Bastardo!" Sophia slaps him so hard his ear rings and his cheek sizzles like frying bacon. "Now get out! Leave us before I hurt you something bad!"

Stanley doesn't quite suppress his smile. "Your email about me really bothered her. Took some work to set her straight."

Sophia hugs Stanley. "How could I believe this sweet man could be so horrible like what you said, with so many wives and diseases?"

"You did," Stanley says, "for a miserable half day."

"But we make up, right?" She kisses him.

"Come on, Stanley, let's talk," Luanne says.

"There's no point. Please, just accept it. You're a bright, attractive woman. You have enough money and lots of options. Move on."

On the drive back Luanne is furious with Ezra. "Why did you interfere? Stanley was going to talk to me, I might've changed his mind. But, no, you had to write that fucking email to her!"

Ezra, ear still ringing, stinging cheek a rich purple, points out that the email was yesterday's work, when sadly he lacked any ability to see into the future.

"And remember you forced me to go with you."

"Oh, shut up, Ezra." After a silence, "What the hell, it's over, isn't it."

"I'm sorry, Lu."

More silence.

"That was some wallop she gave you. You didn't deserve it. Almost"

"Thanks."

"Makes you wonder if they're into S&M."

"Stanley and the Queen of Swat?" says Ezra. "Could be. Nothing more kinky than the furniture biz. Sticks and stones may break their bones, but then you have a nice coffee table."

"That, in a nutshell, is your bloody problem, Ezra. You're still twenty-one."

"Well, gazing back at those days through cataract-colored lenses, I'd say a good time was had by all. At least up to a point."

"Definitely only up to."

"Do you ever wonder—?"

"Never."

"Neither do I."

The car turns into the mini-mall and stops at Ezra's storefront.

"Back to Morro Bay?"

"Little late. I'll find a motel."

"I'd offer you a bed, but then where would I sleep?"

"Stop talking in dialog, especially dialog that's cutely ambiguous. You mean something, say it, be a person."

"Sleep with me tonight."

"No."

"Talk about cutely ambiguous."

"I do want to keep in touch, Ezra." She kisses his cheek. "And please clean up that vile bathroom before it sets off a typhoid epidemic."

Half an hour later Luanne returns. She enters his office with supermarket bags holding bleach, cleaning sprays, a mop, sponges, rubber gloves, an entire arsenal of cleaning tools.

"Okay, I'm crazy," she says. "But your bathroom will never be clean if I don't clean it. And what the hell else do I do with my life today?"

No response from Ezra who's curled up in the overstuffed chair. She realizes his blank look and embryonic position are reminiscent of the Last Days of the Sixth Floor Walkup.

"Ezra?"

He points mutely at his computer screen. She reads an email from someone named Ariadne who asks him to call her about his kidney donation because it's time. He can take the preliminary tests in Los Angeles, but will have to be in New York for the procedure.

"You're donating a kidney?"

Ezra nods.

"Who is she?"

"A friend of Max's."

"That's very generous of you."

"Uh huh."

"I never would've thought."

"Fool you every time."

"Does Serena know?"

He shakes his head.

"Maybe I should tell her."

"Say I did it so there's one thing she'll never get in the divorce."

"Do you still faint at the sight of blood?"

"I faint at the sight of ketchup."

"Yet you're doing this. And you're miserable about it. I'm confused. And please don't tell me it's out of the kindness of your heart."

"You're not the only one who's confused."

"You must have a reason."

"You would think. Feel free to clean the bathroom."

That night Luanne shares his air mattress after all. Later sleepless Ezra senses that she is also awake.

"I figured out the reason," he whispers.

"You were stressed. Don't worry about it. Night."

"I mean why my kidney donation. The reason is Catharsis."

"Huh?"

"For example, my bathroom was filthy, disgusting. Now it sparkles. I never knew the tile was white. It smells like an apple orchard. That's catharsis. Greek Tragedy 101. In dirty, out clean."

"Go to sleep, Ezra."

"Catharsis is why I need to be a donor."

Now Ezra is able to sleep. In the morning he awakens to find Luanne gone. Her note reads, "I'll be in touch. Please keep me informed. Last night was not such a great idea. You are a far better person than I ever suspected. Fondly."

He peels her note from the bathroom mirror, revealing glass that actually reflects. If anything, it does the job too well (how long have those forehead lines been there, that worried pinch between the brows?). Overall, however, Ezra quite likes this enhanced image of himself.

He fills out a long, intrusive donor form online. Five days later he's at a nearby hospital sitting across the desk from a twelve-year-old girl who claims to be a psychologist.

"Mr. Popkin, on behalf of the transplant community, let me start by thanking you. If only there were more people who were equally…well, what word would you use?"

"Noble."

She grants him a tiny smile. "Got it. Noble. Another word?"

"Grateful."

"Okay. Grateful and noble. And, your wife, does she view it the same way?"

Ezra has heard nothing from Serena, though he assumes that Luanne spilled the beans. He's imagined with delight her confused reaction to his Gandhi-like sacrifice.

"My wife is good with it."

"You gave us contact information so we emailed her a few questions. Ms Popkin's comment on you donating a kidney was—" She leafs through papers in a folder. "Quote: 'Didn't go far enough. He ought to donate his entire body.'"

"We're divorcing. People say things."

"She also said you'd had marriage therapy. You denied you were ever in therapy."

"For a few months ten years ago. It doesn't count. Ask her. We laughed over how ineffective the sessions were." Where are steel ball bearings when you need them?

"That would have been Dr. Sidney Fingerman?"

"Sounds familiar. I heard he died."

"In the past twenty-four hours?"

The psychologist removes a thick collection of papers from the folder.

"Emails, Mr. Popkin."

He leaps to his feet. It's hail-mary time.

"Why this inquisition? The facts are simple. Ariadne needs it, I have it. Everything else is commentary." He snatches the papers from her. "I'm a writer, I invent stories. People who confuse fiction with reality ought to get outside more often." He scatters the papers. "My kidney is waiting. I hope you can live with your decision, because someone else might not."

Ezra trudges from the bus stop to his office like a sleep walker. Crossing the mini-mall's parking area he's unaware of the car backing out that nearly hits him.

His neighbor, Mr. Ghupta, calls out, "Ezra! Why such obliviousness? What's wrong?"

"Organ rejection."

"Truly?" Ezra vanishes into his office.

The next day the formal rejection arrives by phone, with letter to follow. Ezra forces himself to call Ariadne. To his great relief she has a backup donor flying in from Detroit later in the week.

"It's outrageous," he moans. "All over the world people steal kidneys left and right. I can't even give mine away."

"I told Max you offered."

"What'd he say?"

"Doesn't believe me."

Shit. Oh well, one less party he won't have to avoid for the next decade. He contemplates moving out of his mini-mall in the dark of night.

"Don't worry, I'm working on him," Ariadne says.

"Will you let me know when it's done? Your transplant?"

"Ezra—of course."

However low his spirits after this phone call, they sink lower when an email arrives from his therapist:

Dr. Sidney Fingerman to Ezra: Termination
Ethical considerations force me to terminate our relationship. I will be happy to supply names of other therapists.

Ezra to Dr. Fingerman: It's okay
I bear no grudge. I did authorize you to use a certain statement as you saw fit. As for all the rest, well, if I can't forgive my therapist how can I forgive others?

I.e. , my wife, the people who pretended to insure my car, fools who label my kidney persona non grata and every amateur who manages to steal and/or sell for major bucks screenplays that are rightfully mine.

To abandon me for ethical reasons at my lowest point strikes me as totally unethical.

Dr. Sidney Fingerman to Ezra: Clarification
You misunderstand. It seems I have a development deal for a motion picture screenplay. My major character is a writer who bears a superficial resemblance to you, but is in fact a composite of several case histories.

Nonetheless our legal people inform me I cannot in good conscience continue our relationship.

May I offer one insight gleaned from this exciting new venture? What you need is not a new therapist but a new agent.

I'll be pleased to put in a word with mine, Brad Klotz, who's said to have an excellent reputation.

Ezra bursts into Brad's office at Talent Central.

"You sold my life on behalf of Dr. Fingerman!"

"Ezra, it's what I do."

"Really, that's your job? In one fell swoop to deprive me not only of my therapist but my life story?"

"First of all, don't flatter yourself—"

"I have his fucking email confession!"

"Okay, we can probably get you a few bucks as a consultant."

"I am not a consultant on my life! I'm living the goddamn thing!"

"There are two schools of thought on that. You're out of

control, Ezra, and it's a shame. But if you barge in here again I'll have your ass locked up till hell freezes over."

"Don't throw 'hell freezes over' at me, you cliché-ridden icy-hearted hustler!"

Ezra shouts this over his shoulder as two security guards hustle him out, one of them a slim female who has no trouble keeping Ezra's feet off the ground.

A message from Luanne awaits him at his office. Has a date has been set for the transplant? He erases the message.

In the days that follow tears rise in him but never emerge. He fears he'll collapse into a sodden heap at any moment. He keeps himself occupied at the computer for hours. He emails multiple letters-to-the-editor. He joins forums in which he has no interest, to give voice to the uninformed. He tweets with abandon and increasing opacity.

He reads books he's forgotten were on his shelves, sometimes spending an hour on a page and writing copious notes in the margins. He sits behind his front blinds peeking out.

So he is primed when the following email shows up:

Sunimitsu Heavy Industries to Ezra Popkin: Welcome!
Congratulations! Thank you for enrolling in Sunglow Entertainment Group's Masterpieces of World Music for an entire year. Each month you are now entitled to download three albums by artists in the categories you have selected: Hip-hop, Reggae and Disco.

Your membership also entitles you to a popcorn upgrade at any Suntainment Multiplex Cinema, giving you the bonus of one Galaxy Size Popcorn for the price of a Super Nova.

Welcome to our family!

> *"Dancing snowflakes, where do you go in summer?"*
> *Masaru Kuriama,*
> *Founder & President, Sunimitsu Industries.*

Ezra rolls up his sleeves, takes several deep breaths and applies fingers to keyboard like a drum roll.

Ezra Popkin to Sunimitsu Heavy Industries:
A Tale of Good and Evil
FOR THE PERSONAL ATTENTION OF FOUNDER & PRESIDENT
MASARU KURIAMA:

As a writer I am all too familiar with corporations run by idiot underlings. It is obvious you have immersed yourself too deeply in philosophy, allowing said idiots to run your own company totally off the tracks.

I urge you to give the following scenario your careful attention.

It concerns one kindly old lady whose mind is not as sharp as it used to be—my mother—and one multinational corporation with the same failing—your baby.

As our story opens, Mom trembles under threat of eviction from the Boston branch of your Silver Gables Retirement Division.

The back story (see attached emails) involves a devoted son three thousand miles away in Los Angeles who has been diligently sending in rent payments to you every month, and a corporate billing center which has been equally diligent in misdirecting them.

The son explains. Pleas. Threatens. All to no avail. So the Heartless Corporation (trite, but here unavoidable) evicts the bewildered widow and mother into the streets. Where the wind-chill factor is colder than the conscience of a multi-national.

The son races across the continent to rescue the dear person who has given him life. Day after day he tramps the cow-path streets of Boston, asking every stranger if he or she has seen a white-haired old lady with a bewildered smile. Who is, perhaps, buttonholing passersby to tell proud tales of Her Son the Playwright.

Meanwhile Mom, her mind unhinged further by the misdeeds of the Heartless Corporation, boards the ferry across Boston Harbor. In the middle of the crossing she leaps into the chill waters, believing it is summertime, and she is young, and her favorite beau is daring her to dive off the pier...

Now let's leave scenario-land and get to the point. Were you to wrongfully evict my mother, could any jury fail to declare the Heartless Corporation guilty of hundreds of millions of dollars worth of pain and suffering? Even billions?

Try me.

Worse, this heart-rending tale would wind up on CNN, Rachel Maddow, a thousand blogs, the TONIGHT SHOW and the front pages of every supermarket tabloid, turning the vast American public against you, your countless subsidiaries and your country.

My mother is occupant #86520-Q. I know you will do the right thing.

Ezra spends half a day rewriting the email, then sends it off with a firm middle-finger jab. The exhilaration of a job well done soon evaporates and once again he peers into the bleakness that is his future.

Several times over the next week Betsiross knocks and calls his name, but Ezra forces himself to stay mute behind his locked door. Mr. Ghupta slips a take-out menu under the door. Chicken korma is circled, with the felt-tipped plea, "Free! Your feedback required on new recipe!"

He emerges only after others in his mini-mall have turned off their lights and gone home to wives, husbands, lovers, children, friends.

At the supermarket he pushes a cart among midnight shoppers while chanting his silent mantra, "I have not become pathetic."

Rent is much on his mind these days. Not his mother's rent, except for delivery problems (between Social Security and an annuity he set up in his heyday she's okay) but his own.

Serena's lawyer is demanding that Ezra stand and deliver. Everything—future residuals, royalties, pension, retirement savings, airline miles, gold fillings, loose change etc., spanning four single-spaced pages.

His own lawyer assures him he will not quite become a pauper, adding with a jolly high-five, "At least not until you get my bill."

An accidental glance at the $1.79 residual check pinned to his bulletin board elicits a long sigh. Once a joke, now a down payment on a Happy Meal.

Time to bite the bullet.

Ezra to Henry Lifshultz, Heating & Air Conditioning:
Moving on
You may rent my office in your mini-mall to a more productive
member of society as of Monday, perhaps sooner. You've been a most
decent landlord (pepper-spraying aside) but I will be moving into a far
more compact space.

I've enjoyed being part of our little community. If circumstances
permitted I would sign a hundred-year-lease and call it a day. But I see
no way to continue on.

There are people here I will miss though I am not man enough to say
goodbye, for reasons too difficult to explain. If anyone asks about my
abrupt departure, please extend my apologies and warm feelings.

Barely an hour after this email goes out Ezra hears a hammering
at his door.

"Open up, Mr. Popkin! It's me, Henry Lifshultz your landlord!"

Ezra shouts back through the closed door and blinds. "What
do you want?"

"Please don't kill yourself! I'll never be able to rent the place!"

"Why would I kill myself?"

"You said in your email."

Ezra unlocks the door and Henry Lifshultz steps in.

"Follow me, Mr. Lifshultz."

He leads him to the computer and brings up the email in
question. "Does that look like a suicide note to you?"

Lifshultz reads. "Absolutely."

"Do you realize how many suicide notes I've written for my
characters? I know how to craft world-class suicide notes. This is a
moving-out note."

"With all due respect, I have to disagree. Look here, where it
says 'a far more compact space.' You think I don't know what you're
talking about?"

"I meant a one-room apartment."

"Then why didn't you say so? Did you have to be so roundabout,
a man like you who can write such beautiful screenplays?"

Ezra collapses onto his chair in despair. "You're right. It's
ambiguous. A simple note to my landlord and I fuck it up."

Lifshultz sits across from him. "It's all right, Ezra, I understand. You've been having problems for a while. Okay if I call you Ezra?"

"Sure. How do you know my problems?"

"This mini-mall has no secrets. Anyway, I've been discussing your situation with some people and maybe we can help you out. Call me Henry, by the way."

Help him out? Ezra's brain goes on high alert. Have Lifshultz and his poker-playing insomniacs anted up enough for a low budget production of *Catman Duo?* A beautiful screenplay, he just said it. Doesn't have to be Paris, it can be Van Nuys. Is this finally Ezra's turn at bat? Welcome, Henry Lifshultz, Heating, Air Conditioning and Deus ex Machina!

"What did you have in mind, Henry?"

"How'd you like to be my night watchman here?"

"Night watchman?"

"I need someone who's always around to keep an eye out, which you happen to be anyway. Maybe also you could take on some light maintenance. I heard how you helped fix up the Thai Massage after immigration swooped through like a pack of Attila-the-Huns. The mechanical touch is said to be a rare thing in your profession."

"I got it by osmosis."

"So what do you say? I'll cut your rent by two-thirds. Plus extra for the maintenance."

A long silence.

"Ezra? Did I insult you?"

"No, I was just running your offer by my people. Well, former people, my ex-wife, ex-agent, ex-partner and ex-son. Apparently it's unanimous. Career-wise, this is the only way to go."

"So we have a deal?"

"Drop the rent by three quarters. And can you manage a new toilet?"

"Done. And if you need extra income, your neighbors here will be happy to throw some work your way."

"They said that?"

"Every one."

"Really?"

"Only promise one thing. No matter how desperate you get, never again will you try to sell a kidney on the black market."

"But I didn't—"

"Thank god."

"That's what they all think?"

"The subject is closed, no one will ever mention it."

With a jingle of bells Henry Lifshultz opens the door and is gone. Ezra cries like a baby.

He has never felt more content. His sleep is untroubled, his days punctuated by tasks of great or little import to which he applies himself with equal dedication. He reads, he watches TV, he naps, he takes walks.

His fellow tenants seek his advice on a wide range of subjects. He has long conversations with Mr. Ghupta about responsibility for global warming. Yankel, of the eponymous Yogurt Shop, begs his opinion about flying saucers in Area 51 when Ezra arrives to change a fluorescent tube.

He has taken to sitting outside his office in a plastic patio chair with a book, greeting strangers as they pass, warmed by how often his friendly, "Good morning," is returned.

After his blood pressure remains a constant thirty points lower he packs away the machine.

Betsiross asks why the word "phonetic" begins with "ph" instead of "f," to his great delight. With his regular guidance her English has been developing rapidly, as has their friendship. He learns that in Thailand she had a husband, a grocery store they ran together and a house, all of which washed away in the floods.

Ezra wonders if he's ready for the direction their friendship is surely headed, alternately wonders if he's kidding himself, then decides not to decide and take each moment as it comes.

Twice a week in his office four other masseuses sit cross-legged in a semi-circle before him for their own English lessons. (Betsiross has hers over burgers or pizza in budget restaurants.)

He delivers dry cleaning in the dry cleaner's van, his PTS vanquished. Buy Ezra wool and he will knit you a scarf.

The only disturbing note is a story he sees on TV about a Greenpeace ship that attempted to interfere with whale hunters. Among those removed from the Greenpeace vessel and placed under arrest are Barry and Bitsy. All diplomatic means are being used to bring them home.

Ezra sighs at his former agent's predicament. Otherwise, do his thoughts ever drift back to screenplays, treatments, dialog and such? Never. This is the stuff local yahoos graffiti on the walls and he covers up with his paint roller.

Koji Catenae, Sunimitsu Heavy Industries to Ezra Popkin: Your payments

I have been asked to extend most warm thanks for the heartbreaking story you have sent to our President and Founder.

Mr. Kuriama would have liked to respond personally. However your tale so moved him that he has isolated himself in a distant monastery, where he composes haiku in praise of his own long neglected but revered mother.

Please contact me so that we may satisfy your every requirement in this matter.

"Now that is one hell of a form letter," Ezra thinks, but he feels no need to reply and henceforth rarely even turns on his computer.

One Saturday evening some weeks later Ezra is taking a customer's dinner order at the Delhi Deli, where he fills in now and then. The customer, a grey-haired man with an engaging smile, glances up from the menu.

"Are you Ezra Popkin, the writer?"

"I'm Ezra Popkin the waiter. Are you ready to order?"

"You're a hard man to locate."

"Sorry, it's been crazy here tonight."

"Len Swiggert, Myopix Films." He hands Ezra his card.

"That's okay, we don't discriminate. Do you need more time?"

"Mr. Popkin, your story is one of the most moving that's ever come across my desk. The adventures of a desperate son searching the city's streets for the elderly mother he's neglected, her attempted suicide by drowning and (with your approval) his last-minute dive into the frozen waters to save her, that will make one hell of a movie. And, of course, you'll write the screenplay."

"Thanks, but I don't do that anymore. May I recommend the lamb jalfrezi? It's outstanding tonight."

"Myopix is a division of Sunimitsu Heavy Industries. Didn't they contact you?"

"Ah." Ezra sits opposite Swiggert. "My story moved Mr. Kuriama into a monastery."

"It had a powerful effect on him."

"And he's instructed you to satisfy my every requirement in this matter."

"I wouldn't say 'every' requirement. But he has taken a personal interest, so you can expect us to be quite generous."

"I remember the word 'every.'"

Swiggert smiles benignly. "What do you want?"

"My every requirement? Go away and never come back. Unless you like our food. Then please do come back, and tell your friends."

"Mr. Popkin, take your time. Think about it. Play with big numbers. You won't be far off."

They shake hands.

Swiggert says, "Is the lamb jalfrezi really outstanding?"

"Go for the chicken tikka. You know, if you guys have the reach you seem to, there are some friends of mine who need a favor."

"Name it, Ezra."

A week later Ezra is pleased to see that the Japanese government has allowed the "Greenpeace 5" to return home. Next Saturday he finds Swiggert again seated in the Delhi Deli.

"What's good tonight, Ezra?"

"You like hot?"

"Hotter the better."

"Let me order for you."

"Fine. And an Indian beer, please. Hope we were able to satisfy your requirement."

"You did. Thank you."

"Any other matter we can attend to, call me day or night. No obligation."

"Let me put your order in. Beer's on me."

"I understand you work best with a partner."

"You were misinformed. I manage quite well on my own these days."

"Japan's top screenwriter is standing by to work with you. Don't worry, his English is pretty good. He can come here or you go there, your call. But I assure you accommodations over there will satisfy your every requirement."

And so the snake entrenched himself in the Garden of Eden and showed up every Saturday night and Ezra grew exceeding wretched. He tells Mr. Ghupta he can no longer wait tables on Saturdays. He snaps at his struggling English students. Conversations with Betsiross dwindle to moody silences.

"You stop liking me?" Betsiross says one evening during dinner in the small Italian restaurant they enjoy.

"How could you think that? You're the one person…"

"One person what, Ezra?"

"Betsi, you're my one person."

"Okay, I take that. Then how come all a sudden you look so…?" She illustrates by scrunching her face into a pained scowl.

Ezra lays out Len Swiggert's temptation and how it's been gnawing away at him.

"Lots money?"

"Uh huh."

"Deal is really kosher?"

"Seems to be."

"You a fucking crazy person?!!"

Her angry exclamation draws the gaze of other diners. But Ezra doesn't see anger across the table, instead discovers something quite different that moves him to his core—the face of a woman he loves.

He puts a finger up. "Excuse me." He extracts Len Swiggert's card from his wallet and calls him. "This is Ezra. I don't have a figure yet, but a ballpark would be enough income to live on the rest of my life more or less modestly…yes, I believe I've heard of the Cayman Islands."

Ezra takes Betsiross's hands and leans across to kiss her.

"Thank you."

"Hah. Sometimes you forget how smart you are."

"I think we have to go back to my place. Right now."

"You need emergency massage?"

"No."

"About time!"

Unwilling to be away from Betsiross for six months, Ezra opts to work in Los Angles with Atushi, his new Japanese writing partner. Swiggert sets them up in an office with a grand view of Downtown and the Pacific. Ezra rents a small apartment for him and Betsiross, but retains his pied-a-terre in the mini-mall.

Two months into the project (and all's well) Ezra receives an email from Stanley:

Stanley to Ezra: OK you told me so
I was a first-class shmuck.

Sophia's ex-boyfriend still had a key to her apartment and he snooped into her computer. When he came across your email warning her about me he went ballistic.

Lorenzo confronted us as we were having dinner at our favorite trattoria. By "confronted" I mean the pair of them began shouting back and forth, arousing the deep interest of the other patrons.

The subject was obvious, to judge by the changing reaction of our audience. First they nodded at me in sympathy, then began glaring and sending obscene gestures my way.

Sophia said later she'd never seen Lorenzo so agitated. What she neglected to mention was that it turned her on. They were back together by the end of the week and I'm barred from that trattoria for life.

This only accelerated the inevitable. It was already becoming obvious I don't belong here. Fortunately my relationship with BunnKumfi continues, and is attracting other interest in my work. I leave Italy the end of the week to rent workshop space and an apartment in L.A.

Can you put in a word with Luanne? She refuses to see me for even one second so I can beg for another chance. She says I disgust her, which is killing me.

Luanne to Ezra: Our mutual ex-partner
Sorry, Ezra, but I'm really not interested in anything Stanley has to say. My life is off in a new direction and it doesn't include the dregs of the last one.

I'm moving back to L.A. to give acting another try. Serena spoke to Stefan, who promises to see what he can do , maybe small parts or voice-overs. Can't ask for a better re-entry into the business. (Guilt? I'll take it.)

Ezra to Luanne: Go for it
But beware of creeps bearing gifts. Keep your bullshit detector on high and your legs together.

Ezra and his Japanese partner turn in the final draft of their screenplay after six months of a frosty but professional relationship. Atushi departs for Japan, with much bowing between the two collaborators, neither of whom cares to see the other ever again.

Ezra and Betsiross set out to buy a home in the Hollywood Hills. He gives the broker only one absolute condition, that the place be architecturally insignificant. After a hundred houses they find one that excites both of them and now launch into furnishing it. Betsiross sees a need for remodeling as well but knows enough to keep quiet. At least until they've settled in for a while.

Ezra's picture is released. He locates few U.S. reviews, not surprising since the film is a limited release Japanese language production set in Tokyo with Japanese actors. A foreign review that he has translated finds the theme "deeply rooted in Japanese folk tales."

The story seems to affect viewers everywhere in the same way: they leave the theatre in a mad rush to contact neglected mothers.

Ezra waits for agents to reach out to him, for the job offers to pour in, so he can dismiss them all with a wave of his hand. He waits in vain. Though credited with original story and shared screenplay for a movie that has become an international phenomenon, he remains without honor in his hometown.

Ezra and Stanley are relaxing in Ezra's mini-mall office, which he's turned into a comfortable retreat with club chairs, a table and chairs and a giant TV. The two men sip cappuccinos from Ezra's brand new commercial-quality espresso machine. Beside it are a variety of cookies and cupcakes, delivered daily. Storekeepers in the mini-mall have learned they are welcome to drop by anytime to refresh themselves.

Stanley himself drops in because having hired a designer and a fabricator he has a fair amount of free time, except when he's running himself ragged during furniture conventions and business trips worldwide.

"I caught Luanne on TV last night," Stanley says with a sigh. "She had two lines."

"I saw it."

"I cried."

"It was a sitcom."

"Ezra, what the hell am I going to do?"

Betsiross comes in from the massage parlor to pull an espresso for herself.

"Maybe you date Babafrichee. Cute girl. Lotsa fun."

"Thanks, Betsiross, but not my type."

"You only got one type, right? Begin with 'L'." She leaves.

"I told Betsi she didn't have to work, but she likes keeping busy," Ezra says. "We're both looking for something different she can do."

They sit in contemplative silence for a while.

"Think she could run a coffee shop?" Stanley says. "If you want to turn this place into the real deal, I'd go in with you."

And that is how Ezra and Stanley become partners again.

Betsiross and Ezra are married on the patio of their new home in the hills. Among those attending are son Max, who caters the event as his wedding gift, Barry and Bitsy, who now run an environmental foundation with seed money from Bitsy's trust fund (their days in an Asian jail have made them less hands-on) and Stanley and Luanne. Also present are Ezra's mother and her new husband, Lester Hemmings, on their way to a Hawaiian honeymoon.

Stanley and Luanne exchange barely half a dozen words for the first couple of hours. But as twilight falls Ezra shows his new bride the pair sitting in Luanne's aubergine convertible talking, and nodding, and smiling at each other. Stanley removes his coat and places it around Luanne's shoulders. Ezra has to look away—the gesture seems as intimate as if Stanley were undressing her.

Ezra's Japanese movie, to which he's happily given no thought in the delightful months of his new marriage, suddenly thrusts itself back into his life. The damn thing is in the running for a Golden Globe Award as Best Foreign Film! As the only local boy involved Ezra is summoned to press conferences, screenings and lunches, where he is pressed for his insights into Japanese film making and folklore.

His movie actually wins, and suddenly Ezra finds himself in broader demand as a spokesman for Japanese film culture. He's on TV morning talk shows, NPR, college campuses and the occasional magazine cover, one of which has him looking distinctly Japanese.

Yet there are still no calls from agents and producers for him to haughtily reject. He's baffled, frustrated, even pissed, until he stumbles across the answer during a cocktail party at the American Film Institute, after participating in a round table discussion on "Anime, CGI and the Decay of the Human Psyche."

He overhears two students discussing him.

"You call your mom after the movie?"

"Uh huh."

"Me, too. But where does Popkin go from here? I mean he

writes Japanese morality tales. And he's old."

"Hear ya. It's like he's trying to screw himself every way possible."

The New York Times Magazine has published an interview with Ezra. He decides this nicely bookends his career. Like a thunderclap, he cancels all scheduled interviews and public appearances and cuts off further contact with the media, Harvard and cineastes online and off.

The headline in Variety reads, "Popkin Pulls a Garbo."

Betsiross proves to be a competent and dedicated manager of the new coffee shop, which thrives from day one.

Ezra and Stanley can usually be found at their regular table, often the only one without a laptop. They discuss politics, their times writing together, the new house Stanley and Luanne bought in the hills of Studio City (for which Serena is pushing a combined media room and display area for Stanley's designs) and everything else.

Now and again Stanley or Ezra will mention that such-and-such a concept would make a great movie. They might even sketch a brilliant opening scene, tossing out ideas and dialog, talking over each other excitedly, Ezra bullying Stanley to see the truth of the matter, sometimes bringing up his ultimate argument, "Who the hell is the one here with the Golden Globe?"